"You surprise me, Angelica," ~~h~~ ~~s~~ ~~d~~ *in a low voice. "Continually and unexpectedly, you surprise me."*

His words left her speechless, yet her body responded with yearning and astonishing warmth.

He reached out and touched her cheek. "I promised myself I wouldn't do this. Not yet." His fingers traced her jawline, lingering on her sensitive skin. His touch was mesmerizing her so, she could neither move nor speak.

"I knew you would feel like cool porcelain," he said softly. "Now let me taste the fire."

He realized he was rushing her, but the bliss touching her brought him was irresistible. He wanted her with a shocking fierceness, and he gathered her closer. He plied her mouth with a quickening rhythm, feeling her respond with each change and movement. When their mouths met, he tasted more than fire. He tasted a need that matched his own. . . .

WHAT ARE *LOVESWEPT* ROMANCES?

They are stories of true romance and touching emotion. We believe those two very important ingredients are constants in our highly sensual and very believable stories in the *LOVESWEPT* line. Our goal is to give you, the reader, stories of consistently high quality that may sometimes make you laugh, sometimes make you cry, but are always fresh and creative and contain many delightful surprises within their pages.

Most romance fans read an enormous number of books. Those they truly love, they keep. Others may be traded with friends and soon forgotten. We hope that each *LOVESWEPT* romance will be a treasure—a "keeper." We will always try to publish

LOVE STORIES YOU'LL NEVER FORGET
BY AUTHORS YOU'LL ALWAYS REMEMBER

The Editors

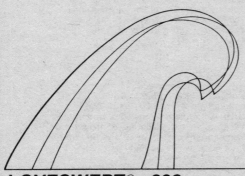

LOVESWEPT® · 298

Linda Cajio
At First Sight

BANTAM BOOKS
TORONTO · NEW YORK · LONDON · SYDNEY · AUCKLAND

AT FIRST SIGHT

A Bantam Book / December 1988

*LOVESWEPT® and the wave device are registered
trademarks of Bantam Books, a division of
Bantam Doubleday Dell Publishing Group, Inc.
Registered in U.S. Patent
and Trademark Office and elsewhere.*

*If you would be interested in receiving protective vinyl
covers for your Loveswept books, please write to this address
for information:*

*Loveswept
Bantam Books
P.O. Box 985
Hicksville, NY 11802*

ISBN 0-553-21949-9

Published simultaneously in the United States and Canada

*Bantam Books are published by Bantam Books, a division
of Bantam Doubleday Dell Publishing Group, Inc. Its trademark, consisting of the words "Bantam Books" and the
portrayal of a rooster, is Registered in U.S. Patent and
Trademark Office and in other countries. Marca Registrada.
Bantam Books, 666 Fifth Avenue, New York, New York 10103.*

For Bev, who has kids of her own . . . and knows.

One

"Please explain why *I* need to rest right in the middle of negotiations," Angelica Windsor whispered fiercely to Dan Roberts as he led her down the hotel corridor, his hand tightly wrapped around her arm.

"Because you're tired," Dan said as he stabbed the Up elevator button. "If you don't like that one, think of it as lunch."

"At eleven in the morning!"

"It beats watching you fall into Garner's trap," he said, shaking his head. "First you seem to be off in space, and then you're losing your temper, against all the rules. You know better than to tell the opposition he got his law degree from a preschool. What's wrong with you, anyway?"

"Nothing," she muttered. Silently she added, nothing except that Dan Roberts was sexy. And she had found herself paying more attention to him than to the delicate business meeting they'd been attending—with near disastrous results. Everything was always wrong when she was with Dan. Fortunately, she had been with him only five times since they had first met, but that was five times too many for her peace of mind.

The elevator arrived. They stepped into it, and she sneaked a glance at him. He was definitely the most attractive man she knew. He was tall and slim, almost to the point of thinness, yet she could easily see the strength under his dark gray suit. He wore round, studious-looking glasses, but they didn't detract from the sharp, rugged planes of his face. His eyes were a deep brown, his nose straight and narrow, and his mouth . . . his mouth was sensual, enticing.

Stop looking at his mouth! Angelica ordered herself. Her relationship with Dan was purely business, always had been, always would be. They had met nine months ago when he had tried to buy the rights to her cousin Diana's latest computer game. Dan's offers had been straightforward and up-front —but then someone had stolen the game from Diana's house. Since Diana had been involved with Dan's brother, Adam, Angelica had accused the two men of stealing the game.

Of course they hadn't, and she had felt like a fool when the real culprit was revealed. Perhaps, she mused as the elevator stopped and they stepped out, if she and Dan hadn't started off on such a very wrong footing, they would now be more friendly with each other. As her cousin's attorney, though, she had had to negotiate with Dan for the sale of Diana's new game to his company, Starlight Software. Unfortunately, the relationship between her and Dan hadn't improved.

This week she had flown up from San Francisco to Seattle, where Dan's company was located, to sit in on the negotiations for the licensing of Diana's game to another company, Mark IV Computers. And he'd just pulled her out of those negotiations because she'd been distracted, not knowing *he* had been the distraction!

Dan glanced worriedly at Angelica as they walked down the hall to the Starlight company suite. She was much too quiet, and wasn't kicking up any fuss about his hauling her out of the room where they had been meeting with Mitch Garner, the representative of Mark IV. That wasn't like Angelica.

She had always mystified him, though. It would be easy to miss the tigress in this tall, willowy, always elegantly dressed woman. But there were subtle clues in the tawny brown of her shoulder-length hair and the fire that flashed in her light green eyes. After their initial dealings over her cousin Diana's game, he had seen her only a few times—once when his brother Adam had married Diana, and he had been the best man and Angelica the maid of honor, twice regarding further legal matters on Diana's association with Starlight, and once more when he had visited Adam and Diana in San Francisco. Each time he had been more attracted to her, more on the verge of suggesting they change their business relationship to one more . . . intimate. Yet each time they had ended up arguing over anything and everything. If he said white, Angelica instantly said black. Most times he didn't know whether to strangle her or kiss her.

Opposites might attract, he thought as he unlocked the door to the suite, but that was as far as it would logically go between him and Angelica. Yet, illogically, the pull he felt for her grew stronger with each disagreement. He wanted her in his bed, but sensed that a temporary relationship would never be enough for either of them. Yet that was the only one they could have.

He opened the door and ushered her over the threshold. The sitting room was spacious and had a small wet bar, refrigerator, and stove behind the far alcove. The bedroom was to the right. On the left was an open connecting door that led to another suite, which he used during the weekdays. Weekends he spent at his home on Nadera Island, one of the San Juan Islands. Angelica was staying in the company suite, and he'd been aware from the moment she had stepped into the room last night that the connecting door, normally a necessary barrier whenever people were staying in the company suite, was instead a nearly unbearable temptation.

She settled gracefully on the sofa and kicked off her shoes. "Okay, Dan, now what?"

"Now you stay out of the picture for a while," he said, shutting the door behind him.

"I beg your pardon."

"Angelica, you were letting Mitch Garner provoke you. I warned you that one of his tactics is to anger the opposition while trying to pull a fast one. You almost lost your temper once."

"I'm about to lose it again. With you."

"I'm going to join Clark and Mitch for lunch." Clark was Starlight's own lawyer. "You, in the meantime, will 'rest.' " He had gotten Angelica out of the meeting by saying she had flown in from San Francisco that morning and was exhausted. It was a blatant lie, as anyone could tell by looking at her. Her eyes were bright—probably with irritation at him—and her skin smooth and lightly tanned. He imagined how soft that skin must feel, and imagined stroking a finger across her cheek just to make sure. Then he would—

Dan cleared his throat and pushed away his lustful thoughts. "Perhaps," he said, "Clark and I could just handle Diana's— "

"No. Diana's my client. And my cousin."

Her words touched several already raw nerves in him. "And she's my sister-in-law. That's the problem with you, Angelica. You have never once trusted me. If you'd care to recall when Griegson stole Diana's game, you'd also recall that I take care of my own as much as you do."

"Dan!"

Angry and frustrated, he ignored her and strode through the connecting door to his room. Dammit, he thought as he passed through the bedroom and on into the bathroom, how did that woman always manage to get to him? She had insisted on attending today's meeting, and he was sure she had done so because she didn't trust him to get a good deal for Diana.

The hell with it, he thought, taking off his glasses and splashing water on his face to cool his skin. That he lived in Seattle and Angelica in San Francisco was probably just as well. Otherwise, she'd always be driving him crazy—in more ways than one.

Drying his face with a hand towel, he walked back into the bedroom. He knew he was hardly ready for lunch, especially under the present tension. Something out of place in the room caught his eye, and he lowered the towel. He stared. Somehow his bedroom had acquired an unusual addition. He hadn't seen it there before he went into the bathroom, but he had been preoccupied. Maybe he was dreaming, he thought wildly. He blinked and rubbed his eyes. He opened them again and stared in shock.

There, lying snuggled in the middle of his bed, was a sleeping baby.

Angelica's hands were still shaking in the aftermath of Dan's anger. She leaned her head on the sofa back and closed her eyes to try to calm herself. She had only meant that the responsibility for Diana's rights in the agreement was hers. But she and Dan had clashed from the beginning. A dozen clichés about not mixing ran through her brain. They were all true about her and Daniel Roberts, she thought.

She knew it was better that they didn't get along. Otherwise, she would have no control with him, for her physical attraction to him was too potent. Losing control scared her. It meant being vulnerable. She had seen what vulnerability could do, and she had vowed never to allow it to happen to her.

Shoving away her disturbing thoughts, she brought herself back to the matter at hand. She would, of course, apologize to Dan for her remark. But what he was asking of her, she couldn't do. She represented Diana, and she *had* to be in on the meetings. It wasn't that she didn't trust Dan. She did, but it was vital to her own sense of self-worth to know that she was doing her job. She had once neglected her responsibilities with a client. The result had been tragic, and she had vowed never to do that again.

"Angelica?" Dan called through the connecting door. "Did you happen to bring any extra . . . baggage from San Francisco?"

She sat up. "What?"

"Did you . . . You better come in here."

Bewildered, she rose from the sofa and walked over to the doorway, stopping on the threshold. Dan was standing in the middle of the room staring at something out of her view.

"What?" she asked again, and poked her head around the doorjamb to see what he was looking at.

A baby was lying on the bed.

She gasped at the tiny sleeping being, then swallowed and said, "It's a baby."

"That's what I thought."

She ventured into the room. "What's it doing here?"

"That was my question."

"But this is your room!"

"It might be my room, but it never had a baby in it before," he said dryly.

"But—"

The baby rolled over onto its tummy.

"He'll fall off!" Angelica yelped, rushing toward the wide bed.

Dan got there first. She instantly changed direction and ran into the other side of the bed, in case the baby rolled that way. Dan was leaning over the bed, his hand hovering just above the baby's back. Angelica sat down gingerly on the edge, not wishing to disturb the baby. It was so . . . little, she thought in amazement, staring at the miniature features topped by a thin thatch of blond hair. She noticed the one-piece yellow sleeper it was clothed in was grimy.

Dan picked up a small piece of paper that had been lying under the child.

" 'I don't want the kid,' " he read in a low voice.

"Oh, Danny," she murmured as tears formed in her eyes. She reached out and touched the baby's small curled fist. The skin was so incredibly soft and vulnerable.

Then she realized how she had said his name in her own moment of vulnerability. She glanced up to find him looking curiously at her, and immediately ducked her head.

He didn't say anything to her, but took the other tiny fist in his own. "Poor little guy."

She forced a smile. "Could be a girl."

He chuckled, then whispered, "Did you notice anything unusual while I was in the bathroom? Did anyone come in here? A maid, maybe?"

"Well, I was in the other room, but I don't think so," she whispered back. "I'm sure I would have heard some noise, at least. Besides, the baby would have woken up or something, if it had just been put there."

"Then it must have already been here when I came in."

Anger suddenly shot through her. "Who would leave a little helpless baby all alone like this? He could have fallen off the bed. What if we hadn't come back when we did? He could have been here for hours while we were meeting with Genghis Khan Garner, and nobody would have known!"

The baby stirred at the rising fury of her voice.

"Sssshh!" Dan hissed.

The baby rolled again, and both of them had their hands ready like wide receivers on a thirty-yard pass. They relaxed when the baby settled back to sleep.

Dan gazed at the infant. The words on the crumpled, cheap white paper swirled through his head, and disgust, anger, and horror rose up in him at the cruelty and callousness of the person who had written it. He would love to have that person in the room right now.

Another thought occurred to him, and he said, "You're the lawyer, Angelica. What will happen to him now?"

"I'm a business lawyer," she said. "So I really don't know for sure, but the note makes it pretty clear he was abandoned. I guess the Welfare Department, or

Family Services, or whatever it's called here in Seattle, would have charge of him."

"What will they do?"

"Give him to a foster home. If one's available."
Fresh tears arose.

"I saw a piece on TV about foster home abuses," he said, remembering his shock. "I had thought *Oliver Twist* didn't happen in this day and age."

"I saw one on the lack of foster homes and how they have to put the kids in institutions." Her shattered expression shocked Dan even further. "I don't want that to happen to this one."

His face hardened with anger. "For once, we are in complete agreement. The little guy deserves better."

The baby stretched, yawned, and opened drowsy blue eyes. Dan immediately shut up, hoping the baby hadn't understood what they'd been talking about.

"Hi," Angelica said softly, after a tense silence. "Have a good nappie?"

The baby smiled, then frowned. To Angelica's complete horror, it let out a wail of indignation. Instinct told her to pick it up. She picked it up. The head seemed to rock on the slender neck, and she supported it with one hand as she brought it against her chest.

"What's wrong?" Dan exclaimed, helplessly holding out his hands.

"I don't know!" She adjusted the small body better on her shoulder. The wails of unhappiness blasted her ear, but she was afraid to move and possibly drop him or her. A nebulous thought about eat, sleep, and cry clicked in her mind. There was only one out of the three the child hadn't done yet.

"The baby must be hungry," she said, and immediately panicked. "What are we going to do? We don't have any baby stuff!"

Dan's eyes widened, then he laughed. "Room service! I'll call room service."

"Room service! Are you crazy?"

But he already had the receiver to his ear. "This is 2015. We need food for a baby."

"A bottle," she said, not sure whether the child was old enough for baby food.

"And a bottle." He listened for a moment. "Send up what you've got. . . .Yes, that was the baby. . . . No, we hadn't thought of that. Gas? Are you sure? . . . Four, eh? Well, that's wonderful. No, I'm single. . . ."

Angelica's growing amusement subsided into confusion. What, she wondered, did gas have to do with the baby? And why did it sound so ominous?

"Well?" she prompted, when he hung up the telephone.

"Well . . ." he began, reaching out to caress the baby's cheek. The cries subsided slightly. "Room service is sending up formula. Five different formulas."

"Five!"

"They asked me which brand we preferred. I said all of them." He added to the baby, "Is that room service or what, Tiger?"

"Would you . . ." She swallowed. "Would you like to hold him while we're waiting?"

He nodded and held out his arms. She fumbled around before finally getting the baby situated. It quieted and stared intently up at Dan. Her arms felt surprisingly empty without the child. Her dress felt wet.

Plucking the damp material away from her chest, she smiled wryly and said, "We forgot about diapers."

"I'll call the front desk to see about that." He grinned. "And valet service for you."

"You've been living in a hotel too long, Dan."

His grin widened. "It beats running to a drug store every five minutes."

She knew there was a phone call they should make, and as an officer of the court she was obliged to do so. She drew in a deep breath. "Dan, we do need to call the police and report this."

He gazed at her, his expression curiously blank. "I know."

"I hate this," she whispered.

"So do I."

After a long, reluctant moment, he reached for the phone.

Two

A short time later Angelica was in her bedroom wondering what clothes to put on. Another good dress was out of the question, so she quickly changed into the slightly rumpled slacks and shirt she had worn on the plane. She had a feeling that with a baby around, rumpled was best.

When she returned to Dan's suite, she found him in his sitting room. She smiled as she watched him wandering around showing the baby the pictures, the furniture, the flowers, anything in an effort to distract the child. It wasn't working, but Dan didn't seem to mind.

She had never seen this gentleness in him before, and it fascinated her. He had always been, at best, distant with her. When they weren't fighting, that is. She had made a fool of herself when Diana's game had been stolen, and she had also gotten an excellent deal for her cousin with Starlight Software. She admitted that she had been rather hard-nosed during the negotiations, but she had only been doing her job. Dan, however, had taken her attitude as a personal affront. Since then, they'd had a kind of Mexican standoff. She knew so little about him, and admitted that she'd never taken the time to discover more. The fierce passion that rose within her whenever they were together frightened her too much.

Dan stopped the tour when he spotted her. He picked up the baby's hand and waved it. The gesture, so innocently intimate, cut painfully at her heart. It hurt to know that doing the right thing might be horribly wrong for the child. Something more nebulous was tied to it, as well, something she couldn't quite define.

"I think it's my turn to change," he said, chuckling as he held the baby away from his chest.

"We could try rigging—"

Somebody knocked on the suite door, and they both sighed with relief.

"The Cavalry" she said.

"One of them."

Dan handed the baby back to her and answered the door. A motherly-looking maid was standing there with several diapers. He'd no sooner let her in when room service arrived, and behind that the police with the hotel manager in tow.

A madhouse immediately resulted with the police officer asking questions, the manager demanding an explanation of the baby's appearance, the waiter fussing over the bottles, the maid advising Angelica about infants, and little "Tiger," hungrier than ever and obviously aware of the chaos, screaming at the top of his lungs.

Dan found himself paying far more attention to Angelica as she gazed at the baby and listened to the maid, than to the authorities. She was beautiful, he thought. And the baby, despite the ear-piercing wails, looked so right in her arms. It felt right, too, watching her like this, as if . . .

"Just a few more questions, Mr. Roberts, the police officer said, "and then we'll take the child to the hospital."

"Hospital!" Dan exclaimed. He was echoed by Angelica.

The officer nodded. "To check out the baby. Then we'll turn it over to the Department of State Social and Health Services. Standard procedure in these cases."

"No!" Angelica said, clutching the baby to her. "This child has been through enough! He needs to be fed and comforted, not poked or have needles shot—"

"Officer!" Dan called loudly over the din. "If the baby only needs to be checked out, why can't a doctor do it here? One of my employees is married to a pediatrician on the staff at St. Mary's. We could have her check the baby. If the least little thing is wrong, of course he would go to the hospital then."

"Well . . ."

Angelica stepped closer to the officer. As if on cue, the baby screamed louder than ever.

"The baby's really hungry," she said, her voice low and persuasive. "It will be hours before the hospital is finished with the examination and they feed him. Will you be with him all that time, Officer?"

Dan didn't know whether the poor man would or not, but the suggestion did seem to make up his mind.

"He certainly sounds healthy," the officer said, smiling wryly. "And I've been in this job long enough to know when to stretch the rules."

Dan strode over to the phone. "One pediatrician coming up."

"Officer, why don't you have the social worker come here, too?" Angelica suggested. Dan's hand stilled over the phone, and he turned to see her smile as she picked up a bottle from the room service table. "I'm sure that person will have questions for Mr. Roberts and me, since we discovered the baby. Also, for the hotel management, since it happened here. In the meantime, I'll just take the baby into the other room to change and feed him . . . or her."

Beckoning the maid to follow, Angelica walked briskly into the bedroom and shut the door with such finality that they all stared at it. Dan hid a smile at everyone else's bemusement. Leave it to Angelica to strike a roomful of people dumb.

He finished dialing, deciding he had been designated "tracker down of all things baby."

Ten minutes later, Dan went into the bedroom and shut the door. He leaned against it and gazed at

Angelica sitting in a wing chair. Serenity lit her features as she held the baby in her arms and watched him suck avidly at the rapidly emptying bottle, his eyes closed in pure bliss. He never would have imagined Angelica Windsor had a maternal streak.

She looked up, and he said, "Jan Williamson, the pediatrician, will be here in about ten minutes. I caught her between rounds."

"One obstacle averted," she said with satisfaction. She nodded toward the maid who was standing next to the chair. "This is Libby. She has six children, and she thinks the baby's about three months old."

"All mine are grown now with their own children." Libby smiled at him before saying to Angelica, "Tilt the bottle higher, so he doesn't get any air in his tummy. He won't like it if he does."

"Him?" Dan asked.

Libby chuckled. "And as proud as he could be of it, too, when I changed his diaper."

"I got in the line of fire," Angelica said cryptically, grinning at the child. She lifted her head and said fiercely, "Dan, we can't let them just take him away without knowing where he's going. What if they shuffle him from place to place, or put him in an institution? I couldn't stand knowing we turned him over to that. If only we knew he was going into loving hands. He's just a little innocent baby!"

The same worries burned in him. "What can we do?"

"Demand to know exactly where and to whom he

is going. We've got a right to that for finding him."
She was silent for a moment, then dropped a quiet
bomb. "And if we don't like what we hear, we demand to keep the child until a proper permanent
home can be found."

He drew in his breath sharply. He and Angelica
knew nothing about taking care of a baby. Neither
of them had even been married—not that marriage
qualified anyone for parenthood. Still, the state probably had all sorts of rules and regulations about
abandoned children.

He stared at the baby, whose eyes were still closed
in infant ecstasy. He had held that child, felt the
helplessness in the tiny body. He and Angelica might
not have experience, he thought, but they had car-
ing hearts, and that had to make up for a lot.

He remembered vividly the look of tenderness in
Angelica's eyes when she had watched him hold the
baby. Although directed at the child, he'd sensed
that that tenderness had in some way included him,
and the shock of electricity that had run through
his body had been savage. He wanted to see that
look again, needed to see it again. For once, they
were in unison, and it had taken a baby to bring
that about.

"Nobody," he said, his teeth clenched, "is taking
him anywhere unless we approve, even if I have to
move heaven and earth to do it."

"You better," Angelica said firmly. "And if he has
to go anywhere, we go with him, one of us holding
him the entire time. Once they literally take him out

of our hands, they've got him, Dan. And it will be almost impossible to help him after that."

Nodding, he strode out of the bedroom, ready to do battle with the system. He knew people in the city government, he thought. He'd call every damn one of them if need be to keep the baby safe from bureaucracy.

Jan Williamson arrived almost immediately. Dan had no sooner sent her on through to the bedroom, when someone else knocked on the door.

He mentally steeled himself to face the person from State Social and Health Services, and opened the door.

Instead, he was confronted with Clark and Mitch Garner, obviously finished with their lunch. Dan launched into yet another telling of finding the baby, as the police officer and hotel manager stood by as silent observers.

"Well, how long is this going to take?" Garner demanded. "We've got a very important meeting to finish."

"I'll get there when I can," Dan said patiently. He refused to desert Angelica and the baby to the social worker. "In the meantime, Clark can work through the details of the agreement with you."

Garner exploded. "Dammit, man, I didn't fly up here from L.A. for you to fool around with some baby! You're stalling, Roberts. We start that meeting now or you can kiss any deal with Mark IV good-bye."

"Good-bye," Dan said coldly.

"What!" Garner gaped at him.

"I said good-bye. You know, so long, adios," he added, in case the man missed the point entirely. "Come back when you can negotiate like a human being."

Garner turned beet-red, then whirled out of the room.

"Good!" Dan, said, slamming the door shut behind him. "Clark, call Mark IV and tell them negotiations have broken down with Mitch Garner, and tell them why. We're willing to reach an agreement, but not through threats and ultimatums."

"Right," Clark said.

As Dan saw his lawyer off, he decided State Social and Health Services didn't stand a chance. Then it occurred to him that he would have to tell Angelica *he* had blown the deal. And after his scolding her for nearly losing her temper! He cursed aloud, and at the same time a knock sounded on the door.

"Look out, State Social and Health Services," he muttered grimly, and opened the door.

To his shock, he faced a mountain of domineering humanity. His first thought was that Mitch Garner was a piece of cake compared to this. The stern, no-nonsense face could have been male or female, and the only way he knew it was the latter was from the tight iron-gray curls framing it. Several names immediately popped into his head: Steamroller; Drill Sergeant; Tyrant; Sister Agnes the Terrible from Second Grade.

"Martha Canfield, State Social and Health Services," the mountain said in a deep clipped voice.

Dan instantly decided to skip the mental girding of his loins and go right for the steel truss. Heaven help him if this one was anything like Sister Agnes.

He took a deep breath and smiled. "Come in."

"His heartbeat is perfect, his internal organs are where they should be and the size they should be, and his lungs are super."

"Are you sure?" Angelica asked anxiously.

Jan Williamson chuckled. "Did you hear him scream in outrage while I examined him? Healthy babies have a lusty, strong cry. Since they can't tell us what's wrong, it's the best sign we doctors have of any problems." She rubbed her ear and smiled. "He's about as healthy as they come. His motor reflexes and size indicate he's about three to four months old. You know, I've seen more abandoned babies than I care to think about at St. Mary's, and usually they show some sign of neglect. But he doesn't have any."

Holding the now contented baby, Angelica wondered about the mother who would take good care of an infant, and then callously dump it in a hotel room with no precautions for its safety. Unfortunately, of the two people who would know, one wasn't present, and the other was too little to give any further clues.

"Could he have been kidnapped?" Libby asked, still hovering.

Angelica, grateful for the maid's reassuring presence, replied, "I would think the police would have told us if there had been a kidnapped baby. Besides, the note makes it pretty clear he's been abandoned."

Libby nodded.

"Well," Jan said, sitting down on the edge of the bed and pulling a clipboard of forms onto her lap, "you've got yourself a good one."

Angelica stifled a sigh of relief that the first obstacle of the hospital had been avoided. But she knew the next obstacle was yet to come.

Once she had lost a child to the system, she thought bitterly. Never again.

The bedroom door suddenly swung open, and a large woman marched in.

"*Miss* Martha Canfield, State Social and Health Services," she said brusquely. "The young man said the baby was in here."

Angelica narrowed her eyes at the woman's abruptness. Dan followed behind the social worker, his expression hard and set. She tightened her hands around the baby.

"Well, he looks healthy enough," Miss Canfield said.

"Quite healthy," Angelica snapped. "And fed, and cleaned and changed."

"So I see."

The woman stared at her, clearly sizing her up for something. Angelica set her jaw and stared back. Dan came to stand next to her chair, and she drew strength from his silent support.

"Mr. Roberts has already explained about the baby," Miss Canfield said. "And I've seen the police report.

But I'll need a statement from you, Ms. Windsor, and a report from you, Doctor, then the baby and I will be on our way."

Angelica rose awkwardly from her chair. An armload of baby did not allow for proper body language, she decided, and she needed all her tools of argument at the moment. Besides, she would not use the child as a shield or prop. Her gaze met Dan's, steady and sure, and she knew she could trust him to hang on to the baby at all costs. She carefully transferred the child into his arms. His hands touched hers in the process, and she felt strength and comfort combined with an underlying sizzle of awareness. The baby gazed up at them in round-eyed wonder.

"Don't let go of him for anything!" she whispered, then turned around and faced the confident Miss Canfield. "And where will the child be going?"

"To a temporary accommodation. Until we can find out something more about his circumstances."

"Temporary?" Angelica echoed. "Temporary what?"

"I can't divulge that kind of information," Miss Canfield said frostily.

"We're concerned for his welfare," Angelica said, "and we want to know if you are taking him to a good home, a loving home."

The woman hesitated, and it was all Angelica needed to confirm her suspicions.

"You don't have one available, do you? Your temporary 'accommodation' is some kind of institution, isn't it?"

"We'll take care of the child—"

"That's not care!" Angelica exclaimed. "Look, we're

willing to keep the child here until you have a good home ready for him."

"You're not qualified."

"Then approve us!" Angelica snapped. "Mr. Roberts is a respected businessman of this city, and I am a lawyer licensed to practice in this state. We'll sign anything, do anything you want, but we won't give this child to you unless we are fully satisfied with the arrangements."

"Now calm down," the woman began.

"I will not calm down!" Angelica said fiercely. "If I have to, I'll file a very public lawsuit on this child's behalf—"

"Lady!" Miss Canfield suddenly bellowed. "I'm on your side!"

The loud voice startled the baby to instant tears and cries. Angelica hurried to Dan's side and patted the baby on the back.

"It's okay, Tiger," Dan cooed, rocking the infant. To Angelica, he whispered, "Dammit, you did it again."

"No, I didn't. She's on our side. Hush, sweetie, everything's fine."

She smiled with pleasure as the baby's cries dwindled into soft sniffling.

"Obviously, he likes the two of you," Miss Canfield said, drawing their attention. She commandeered an armchair and settled her bulk into it. "I'm on your side, believe me. We've got a terrible shortage of foster homes in the city right now, and there's nothing I'd like better than to leave the baby with willing people. But there are a number of problems. . . ."

"Whatever you need, we'll do it," Dan said, tilting his head to glance at the infant snuggled against his shoulder. "I like this little guy very much."

The baby smiled at him, and Dan proudly smiled back. Angelica smothered a grin of her own. One thing that was becoming more obvious to her was that she liked Dan. Well, she thought, if a baby liked him, he couldn't be all bad.

Miss Canfield nodded. "The last thing I want to do is put this baby into a hospital until I find even a temporary foster home for him."

"A hospital will only keep him for a day or two at most," Jan Williamson said.

"True. And the alternative gives me nightmares." Miss Canfield looked sternly at Angelica and Dan. "So the two of you want to take care of the child for a while."

They nodded.

"Both of you together."

Angelica glanced at Dan, then said, "Yes."

"Mr. Roberts and *Ms. Windsor.*"

"Ahhhh . . ." Panic-stricken, Angelica realized they wouldn't give a small baby to a single man. And she wasn't a resident of Seattle. Because of a technicality the child would be put into a temporary foster home or worse. She'd seen the devastation a legal technicality could cause. She couldn't allow that, she thought in despair. An idea popped into her head, and hoping against hope she blurted it out.

"We're engaged!"

The room was deathly silent. Although she'd said

them, her words shocked Angelica as much as everyone else. Swallowing hard, she refused to look at Dan. She didn't dare. His body was totally still and she could easily imagine what he was thinking. She would explain to him later, she thought, as she kept her gaze steady on Miss Canfield. Surely he wouldn't kill her for lying like this, not if it got them temporary guardianship of the baby.

"I see," Miss Canfield said. "When's the wedding?"

"At the end of the month," Angelica said, terrified that everything would collapse if she didn't name a date. Fortunately, the lies were coming more easily. "I—I'm living here now. You see, I'm from San Francisco. In fact, I'll be keeping a residence there, since I have a number of California clients. But I will be moving my main office here, after Dan and I . . . after the wedding. I certainly hope this won't cause any problems."

"Well, it's a little unusual . . ."

"This is a temporary care situation," Dan reminded the woman.

"If it will help," Jan added, "I've known Dan for several years, and I can write a statement for you. Also, as the examining doctor, I would recommend that for the baby's well-being, he should stay here until more permanent arrangements can be made."

"That will certainly carry a good deal of weight with my supervisor," Miss Canfield said.

Bless Jan, Angelica thought in relief. And bless Miss Canfield. She wasn't nearly as bad as she looked. Aloud, she said, "Well, now that's settled."

"Not quite." The woman smiled bleakly. "First of all, this is a hotel, not a residence."

"We're buying a place." Hell, Angelica thought, if she'd gone as far as getting Dan engaged, she might as well go all the way.

She nearly choked on her words, though, when she heard a low angry sound coming from his tight lips.

"It's the immediate residence that counts," the social worker said.

"I have a lease with the management for this suite," Dan said, the relief in his voice clearly audible. "They call this an apartment. Does that help?"

"The hotel rents several of these as permanent residences," Libby added. "I know they qualify as that for the city's purposes, so wouldn't they do the same for this? They have cooking facilities."

"I also have a home on one of the islands," Dan added.

"Out of our jurisdiction, I'm afraid. But if this is one of your permanent residences . . ."

"It is. I'm here more than I am at my house."

"I think I can slide that one by," Miss Canfield said. "Now, have either of you had any experience with babies?"

"Would on-the-job training count?" Dan asked, with a straight face.

"Baptism of fire?" Angelica added.

"We'll learn as we go?"

"Jan is a phone call away?"

"We promise not to drop him?"

The baby gurgled and swung his arms.

Jan and Libby laughed . . . and so did Miss Canfield. Angelica stared in amazement as it seemed to boom out of the large woman.

"I like you two," she said, when her amusement subsided.

"Thank goodness," Angelica murmured.

"Thank someone else that you didn't blow it," Dan muttered.

"Be nice," Angelica whispered sweetly. "We're engaged."

Dan didn't have to open his mouth. The expression in his eyes said all too clearly what he was thinking. It was an exercise in bravery to keep the smile on her face.

"In spite of all the rules this job requires," Miss Canfield went on, "it also requires a good deal of flexibility. With kids outrunning family home situations, this little guy doesn't stand much chance without you. You don't have any experience with babies, but the truth is, if nature had brought you the baby in the normal fashion you wouldn't be any more knowledgeable than you are now. In your favor, you have a doctor to vouch for you, the hotel meets city regs for residence apartments—"

"And provides room service," Dan said.

"I should be so lucky. Also, you're well established, engaged, and can provide the child with what we like to think is the ideal environment for children. And I have the strong feeling that this little one couldn't be more safe or well-cared-for if Dr. Spock were volunteering for the job."

"We'll put Dr. Spock in the shade, Miss Canfield," Angelica vowed.

"Call me Martha." She wagged a finger. "No promises, mind you. And it will only be temporary. Now you'll need a crib. . . ."

Angelica held out her arms. "Give him to me, Dan, and go get a crib. And sheets. And blankets. And diapers, and clothes, and toys. A stuffed bear. Every baby should have a Teddy. And a baby care book! We'll need it."

Dan grinned at her. "Your credit card or mine?"

Three

"You bought all this?"

Dan laughed at Angelica's stunned expression, as she gazed at the piles of packages and boxes that had just been carried into the suite.

"I. Magnin loves me," he said, dismissing the two bellhops with a large tip.

"I would say so."

He was proud of himself. No sooner had they received approval as temporary guardians from State Social and Health Services than he was out the door to the nearest department store. In fact, his shopping had turned into a race against the store-closing, and he still wasn't sure he had won.

"How did you get a fully assembled crib out of them?" Angelica asked, setting the baby inside it.

"A lot of fast talking. Fortunately, the department store manager I asked to help me believes in complete customer satisfaction."

She began opening packages. "Omigod! Dan!"

Laughing, she held up a tiny pair of blue satin sneakers and a Mariner baseball outfit. He grinned, and her hands seemed to fly over the bags to discover more baby paraphernalia.

It was amazing, he thought, how united they had been today. If someone had asked him just this morning when he and Angelica would get along, he would have made reference to hell freezing over. He hoped the devil had electric socks.

"I got some formula," he said. "And those disposable bottles. Do you think they'll be okay?"

Her hands stilled and she looked up in bewilderment. "I don't know."

He gazed blankly at her for a moment, then realized they had truly been left alone with a baby. Nobody was there to advise them or help them figure out what the child wanted. Suddenly, he felt as lost as she looked.

He gazed at the baby, who was cooing and gurgling while trying to catch his tiny toes. What if the bottles were all wrong? What if there was something important he had forgotten? What if the baby became sick from the oversight? Now, after all the tension and excitement, the implications of his actions were setting in. He had the care and responsibility of a baby. Jan had left a list of instructions, added to by Libby and Martha Canfield. Still, he and Angelica were such raw recruits.

"I'm scared."

For an instant, he thought he'd spoken aloud, then he realized it was Angelica.

"I really thought I was doing the best for this baby

today," she continued in a whisper. "But now I'm scared to death that I've made a big mistake and he's going to pay for it."

"That certainly makes me feel a whole lot better," he said dryly.

"You don't understand, Dan. You reacted from the heart today. I don't know if I did."

"What?" He frowned. "What are you talking about?"

Absently clutching a miniature. *Playboy* T-shirt, she said, "Once I made a terrible mistake that involved children, and I don't know if I was trying to make up for that today. I hope not."

He could sense the deep pain within her, and it shocked him. Angelica was beautiful and sophisticated, strong-willed and stubborn. He'd never considered that anything could hurt her. And yet it had, and he was seeing it.

He wanted to touch her, hold her, but he could easily sense the rigidity in her, and knew that if he did she would shatter against him. Instead, he asked gently, "What happened?"

She let out a long breath. "I hadn't been in practice very long when a good friend asked me to represent her in a custody suit for her children. Well, it was bitter, and I was textbook experienced, and I lost the case."

"Lost?"

"Yes. My friend neglected to tell me about several things, and when they came out in court, I was unprepared to defend against them." Her voice caught, and she ran her fingers through her dark hair to calm herself. "It was horrible to watch those children taken away from her, doubly horrible to know I was responsible—"

"You weren't responsible," Dan broke in.

"Yes, I was." She glared at him for arguing. "I knew better, but I let her talk me into defending her out of ego. I went into business law after that, and specialized in contracts. Money and fine points were at stake, not people. I thought I'd buried it. . . ."

"Until today," he said, suddenly understanding why she had been so fierce about keeping the baby.

She had opened a door enough to give him a glimpse of the real Angelica Windsor. He wondered how much more of her was unknown and decided there was probably a great deal. And he wanted to learn all of it.

"I think your heart's in the right place," he said, smiling at her.

"I hope so," she muttered, "because I feel like my brain was out to lunch."

She was already closing the door on him, and regretfully, he let it shut—for the moment.

Suddenly she groaned. "I forgot about my practice!"

He started laughing. He never would have thought she would forget business for a baby. "Can you work out of here temporarily?"

"I suppose I could for a while." She shook her head and grinned. "As long as I have a telephone, a computer, and some of my files sent up, I can probably manage. I'll have to."

"You can use anything at my office," he offered. "In fact, anything you need, I'll arrange courtesy of Starlight Software."

"Thanks. Well, I suppose we should move this stuff into my room, so I can get him into bed."

"*Your* room?" he repeated in astonishment.

"Yes." She frowned at him. "Where else would he sleep?"

"How about *my* room? After all, I'm his guardian, too."

"Dan, don't be silly."

"I'm not being silly."

"Well, I'm the woman."

"Angelica, being a woman doesn't mean you can provide better care."

"It doesn't mean I can't."

"I feel responsible," he said, shrugging helplessly. He didn't know if he could explain to her how he felt about the baby. Something inside him insisted that he take an active part in the child's care. Their united front clearly had some shaky foundations. Running his hand through his hair, he said, "Look, why don't we put the crib in the sitting room between my bedroom and yours? It's a fair compromise."

She hesitated for a moment, then asked, "Do you think we'll hear him?"

"I don't know," he said, wondering if the baby's cries would penetrate his sleep. "But people do have separate nursery rooms for their babies, so I suppose it's okay."

Hours later, Dan lay wide awake, his ears attuned to the least sound coming from the sitting room. For the thousandth time, he heard a slight rustle of sheets, and his stomach instantly tensed as he waited for the inevitable cry from the baby. It hadn't happened yet, he reminded himself, and tried to relax. His body refused to obey him, despite the exhaustion from his lack of sleep. Stifling a groan, he rolled over onto his stomach. Every little noise the baby made in his sleep was like a gunshot, startling and deafening. He wondered of Angelica was having the same problem.

He tilted his head so he could just see the open door in the darkness. Beyond the sitting room was Angelica's bedroom. He knew her door was open, too. The baby was only part of his restlessness, he admitted. He'd wanted Angelica from the beginning, and to have her lying in bed just a few yards away. . . She had the ability to infuriate him one moment, and make him laugh the next. She had called him Danny, and nobody, not even his mother, had the audacity to do that. And yet he liked hearing it from her lips.

She had said they were engaged.

He had realized she'd said it to make a stronger case for their temporary custody of the baby, yet it had unnerved him. The idea of being engaged to Angelica, and then married to her, sharing his bed with her every night, taking care of their child . . .

A snuffle followed by a thin cry caught his attention, and he bolted upright. No false alarm this time, he decided, and grabbed his glasses off the nightstand. Getting out of bed, he struggled into his robe, then rushed into the sitting room. As he flipped on the brass floor lamp next to the door, he could see Angelica already at the crib, lifting the baby into her arms. He stopped and stared at the breathtaking sight of her cheek touching the baby's as she soothed him with low murmurs. Her robe was open, and the white cotton nightgown she wore was expensive and incredibly sexy, hinting at her curves, rather than revealing them.

"Angelica," he whispered.

Angelica looked up at the sound of her name. Dan stood just inside the threshold of the sitting room. His robe exposed a deep V of furred, muscled chest before being belted closed at his waist. The robe's hem ended at his knees, revealing strong bare calves and feet. She wondered if he wore anything underneath the bathrobe.

A heavy mist curled through her at the thought. Unable to stop staring, she watched him walk toward her. He stopped by the side of the crib, so close to her that she could feel the heat of his body. He didn't say a word, and she couldn't seem to find her voice to protest his closeness. She sensed that he was going to kiss her. He lifted a hand as if to touch her, and she was helpless to stop him. Her gaze was riveted to his mouth as he slowly bent down. . . .

The baby squirmed, bringing her back to reality.

"I've got him, Dan," she said, finding the strength to turn away. She wasn't sure if she should be grateful or frustrated at the baby's presence. "Go back to . . . sleep."

He shook his head, as if clearing it. "It's okay. I've been awake. Who could sleep with all the noise he's been making?"

She smiled. "And I thought it was just me. The instructions say both ends should be taken care of. I'll change him, and you get his bottle."

"Let me change him," Dan said, holding out his arms. "I haven't done it yet."

"That's okay. Just get his bottle."

"Angelica, are you going to fight me on everything?" he asked in exasperation, lowering his arms.

She bit back a retort and said calmly, "I wasn't fighting with you. I only meant that each of us could take care of one of the jobs. Why do you *always* turn my words into a fight?"

"I wasn't. Look, why don't we change him together?"

She frowned, glancing down at the baby. He wasn't screaming, just fussing a little. "Okay. Get a diaper."

"Right."

She laid the baby down on the floor and knelt next to him as he kicked his feet. The room seemed to dip, and she swallowed to dispel her sudden light-headedness. She'd done all-nighters at law school and felt more wide awake than this.

Dan returned with the diaper and knelt beside her. "Now what?"

"Unpeel the tape and pull off the diaper."

She unsnapped the baby's brand-new one-piece Izod sleeper and pushed it up past his waist. Lord, she thought. Izods for the Yuppie baby. She loved it. Nodding at Dan, she peeled back the tape on her side at the same moment he did his. The baby waved his arms and smiled, clearly enjoying the attention. An odor, distinctive and strong, rose up from the diaper. Angelica immediately reclosed it.

"You know, you're right, Dan," she said in a rush. "You really should change this diaper—"

"Oh, no, you don't," he said. "I saw what was in there."

"But I've done it once already." She didn't add that it had only been wet that time.

"Well, you're on a roll, and I wouldn't want to spoil that," he said magnanimously.

The baby began to fuss again, the novelty of lying on the floor having worn off.

Angelica sighed. "Do it together?"

"With a lot of baby wipes."

They managed together to get a new diaper on the baby. They also used an entire box of wet cloths to do it.

Angelica shuddered as she gingerly picked up the offending garment. Arm outstretched, she got up and desposited it in the farthest wastebasket. She couldn't quite believe it was three o'clock in the morning and she was changing diapers . . . and actually liking it.

"If Mom could see me now," she muttered.

She helped Dan get a bottle ready and bit back a plea to be allowed to feed the child. She knew he wanted to do it. Once he and the baby were settled in a plush armchair, she sat down opposite them and watched him feed the infant. She liked watching him, she admitted. His movements seemed so sure and confident, while she felt clumsy and awkward handling the baby. Oh, well, she thought, she made up for it with enthusiasm.

As she continued to gaze at Dan, she began to

wonder what it would be like to feel those hands, so gentle with the tiny being they held, coursing down her body. Those long, tapered fingers finding her breasts, her waist . . . lifting her, turning her . . .

He looked up at her, and she froze in horror that her thoughts had been read. He smiled, not a smirk of knowledge, just a genuine smile of respect and gratitude. She realized an unspoken truce existed between them—if only a momentary one. It had started with the baby, and it hurt to admit that when the baby was gone, the truce would be gone too.

"How do we manage to do the bottle together?" he asked. "Shall I pass him over halfway?"

"I don't think he'll be happy about that," she said. "You keep him for this one."

He nodded.

She was silent for a moment, listening to the quiet of the night. "Doesn't it feel like we're the only people awake in the world?"

He chuckled. "Tiger here probably delights in that."

She suddenly realized that Dan might be seeing someone, or even be truly engaged to a woman who would not be too happy with a second fiancée. Dammit, she thought. Her cousin had never mentioned anyone was with Dan, but then her cousin might have felt it wasn't her business. "Ah . . . I hope this won't cause too much disruption in your private life, Dan."

He was silent for a long moment. "There's nothing to disrupt."

A strange feeling of relief ran through her.

"And you?"

She tensed, then shook her head.

"I see. Well, Tiger, looks like you're the only complication around here. I wish I knew his name."

"To the authorities he's 'Baby John Doe' " she said, glad the subject had been changed.

Dan grinned. "We're his temporary guardians, so why can't we give him a temporary name?"

She liked the idea. In fact, she had a perfect name. "How about Blaine?"

"Blaine!"

"Sure."

"Bl-ainnnne." He drew it out comically.

"Blaine," she said firmly. "I love the name. I always thought that if I had a little boy I would name him Blaine."

"Blaine's . . . okay." Dan's smile held a hint of a smirk. "Now Christopher is a great name. Sturdy, plain, straightforward."

She made a face. "He sounds like a wallflower at the Harvest Dance. Blaine has more pizzazz, more spice."

"Now he sounds like an ad for Mexican food." He turned to the baby cradled in his arms. "So what do you think, Tiger? Christopher? Or Blaine?"

A rude noise erupted from the baby's diaper as if in answer.

She and Dan looked at each other, then burst into laughter.

"You have to be over twenty-one to vote, kid," she said to the baby.

"Are you going to budge from Blaine?" Dan asked.

"No. Are you going to give up Christopher?"

"Not if Blaine's the alternative."

"I think there's a law against arguing at this hour," she said, flopping back in her chair. "Now what?"

"Flip a coin."

She gasped. "Danny! We cannot flip a coin to decide a baby's name!"

He grinned lopsidedly at her. "Why not? It's fair, and each of us has a fifty-fifty chance of giving the child his name."

"It sounds too sensible, so it makes me suspicious as hell."

"Lawyers don't know what common sense is."

"Very funny."

"Just get the quarter."

"Right."

She went into her bedroom and returned with a coin.

"Heads, Christopher. Tails, Blaine," Dan suggested.

"I can't believe we're flipping a coin for a baby's name," she muttered, and flicked the quarter into the air.

She missed catching it on its downward journey, and it rolled under the coffee table. Scrambling on her hands and knees, she edged under the table and peered at the coin.

"Damn," she muttered.

"What does it say?" Dan asked.

She crawled out from under the table and sat up. She gazed at the baby, who gazed back as he avidly sucked on the nipple of the bottle.

She smiled. "Hi, Patrick."

"Patrick!"

The baby grinned around the nipple and stretched his hand in her direction. Dumbfounded, Angelica looked up at Dan.

"I just threw that out as a joke, to tease you," she said slowly. "But do you suppose it's his real name?"

"It's a common enough name," he said, staring at the baby. "In any case, he likes it."

"Well, so much for flipping a coin," she said, and took the baby's fingers in hers. "Hi there, Patrick. I guess you do get a vote after all."

"It fits," Dan said. "Hearing it, I can't imagine him being called anything else." His voice dropped lower. "Just as I can't imagine you being named anything other than Angelica."

The way he said her name sparked a sensual awareness deep inside her. She wished she could think of something pithy to say that would dispel it, but instead all she had was a lame, "And Dan fits you."

"Then we're Dan and Angelica and Patrick."

The trio of names hit her like an express. They sounded right together. Her mind automatically carried it one step further.

They sounded like a family.

"Dan? I can't find any socks! Did you get socks for Patrick?"

Dan forced his bleary gaze away from the hypnotic dripping of the coffeemaker in Angelica's kitchenette. Babies should only be found by people who suffered from chronic insomnia, he decided.

Finally rousing himself enough to answer, he called out, "Yes. They're somewhere in that stuff."

"I can't . . . Never mind."

Straightening from the counter, he stared down at his own bare feet and wished he had the energy to get his own socks. He'd managed a shirt and pants so far, and he figured he ought to be grateful for that. It might be as far as he got today. Little Patrick had gone back to sleep right after his bottle, only to wake up around six-thirty, an hour ago. At least he'd joined the baby in slumberland for a few hours.

He found it hard to believe that just yesterday morning he had arisen to silence and privacy. This morning had been all noise and bustle, with no thought to whose space was whose.

The truth was, he kind of liked it.

Angelica came around the corner of the kitchenette just as the last of the coffee dripped through. She looked fresh as a daisy compared to him.

"I hope," she said, "that coffee is loaded with caffeine. Megagrams of it."

"We can but pray," he said, getting out a mug for her. He poured the coffee—strong, hot, black coffee. As he handed the mug to her, he realized both her hands were free. "Where's the baby?"

"In his crib, talking to Bryant Gumbel." She pointed behind her with her thumb as a grunt came from the sitting room. "Can't you hear him?"

Dan grinned as he listened to Patrick coo and yip at the host of the "Today" show. "He probably wants to get hold of the guy and shred that polished image."

A worried look came into her eyes. "Miss Canfield . . . Martha's . . . coming today. I don't know when, but I want all of us to look perfect."

"He's been here one day, and we haven't lost him or dropped him. We're not doing too badly."

"True. And look at all our on-the-job training."

"We've kept our cool, and managed." He sipped his coffee, and instantly felt a pulse return to his body. "I might be cool, but I'm getting too damn old to go without sleep."

"Oh, I don't know," she said, smiling gently at him. "You have that world-weary Indiana Jones look. Just the thing to impress Mitch Garner when you continue the negotiations today."

"Ahhh . . ." Damn! He'd completely forgotten about telling her negotiations had broken down with Mark IV. He took a deep breath, gazed straight into her eyes, and said, "Mitch won't be around to see it."

She frowned. "What do you mean?"

"I lost my patience with him and broke off negotiations," he said into his mug.

"You lost—" She stared at him. "After lecturing me about getting emotional, you lost your *patience*?"

"My temper," he mumbled in correction, and explained what had happened.

Angelica smiled evilly. "Well, well . . ."

"You said you wanted to look perfect for Martha," he reminded her. "You better get started."

A pretty flush covered her face. "Do I look that bad?"

She looked warm and soft and sexy in her green sweater and jeans, he thought. Her hair was pulled back, and he had the sudden urge to kiss the satiny flesh of her neck.

"Wellll . . ." he began neutrally.

"We'll talk later," she promised, and disappeared with her coffee.

He sighed with relief as he watched her go. Deciding he needed nourishment before he faced one of Angelica's talks, he ordered breakfast from room service, then joined the baby in the sitting room.

"How's shore leave treating you, buddy?" he asked Patrick, who was dressed in a sailor outfit.

Patrick laughed, while trying to pull his socks off.

"First you've got to find a girl, then you start taking off your clothes," Dan said, and lifted the baby out of the crib. "Let's talk about the birds and the bees. I think you need a lesson, son."

He played with the baby until room service arrived. He was mildly surprised to feel almost human. Must be the baby, he thought, remembering a saying about children keeping one young. He certainly didn't feel young, but at least he was awake. With food, he might even feel alive. He hoped.

After dismissing the waiter, he called Angelica and sat down at the table with Patrick on his lap. The baby instantly dropped his rattle and reached for everything, and Dan patiently moved silverware and china out of his reach. He picked the rattle up and handed it to the child, and it went right to the mouth. Unfolding the newspaper, he decided that all the craziness wasn't so bad. In fact, he enjoyed the baby. And he had seen a side of Angelica that surprised and intrigued him.

He'd have to do something about that, he thought.

He scanned the front page, then froze when he read *Baby Found In Hotel* headlining a brief article. He realized it must have been released by State Social and Health Services to entice someone to come forward with knowledge about the baby. He tightened his hold on Patrick as he began to read the article.

One sentence instantly leaped out at him: *Daniel Roberts, prominent Seattle businessman, and his fiancée, Angelica Windsor, discovered the male infant in Roberts's hotel room. . . .*

He had been angry with her yesterday about the engagement business, but he'd understood why she had done it. In fact, he wasn't sure whether he had been angry that she'd said it . . . or that there was no truth to it. But he'd never considered any real consequences to the "engagement" until now.

The telephone rang in his room. His stomach churning, he went to answer it.

"Hello?" he said cautiously, shifting Patrick, who was trying to eat the telephone cord, to his other hip.

"Daniel, what's all this about finding a baby, and being engaged, and why didn't you call me right away?"

Dan closed his eyes. One big consequence he hadn't expected was on the other end of the line. He drew in a deep breath and opened his eyes.

"Hi, Mom."

Four

"When is the wedding?"

Angelica stifled a grown at that eternal question and rushed to answer it. "We haven't set a date yet."

The reporter from JMB-TV in San Francisco looked disappointed at the neutral reply. She ought to be used to the question by now, Angelica thought in frustration. Every media article about Patrick had played up the ready-made family angle because of the "engagement." And that meant a lot of questions about the impending nuptials. Since the first little article had appeared five days ago, the press had clamored for interviews. Martha Canfield had asked her and Dan to participate, in an attempt to get more information from someone about Patrick. So far no one had come forward. The press, however, was still jamming the sitting room with people and equipment every day. In fact, several TV stations and newspapers in San Francisco had picked up on the Seattle coverage and now wanted to carry the story because of Angelica's ties to that city.

Forcing herself to keep smiling for the camera, she glanced at Dan who was seated next to her on the couch. His smile held a hint of smugness. She supposed he was entitled. So far he'd been the focus of a hail of questions and congratulations. Clearly, he was enjoying her turn on the rack. That he hadn't killed her yet was a miracle.

One little lie had snowballed into an avalanche of deceit. It could only happen to her, she thought in disgust. Her life had become a roller coaster ride of confusion, awkwardness, exhilaration, and exhaustion. She knew things wouldn't be easier when the media left and she and Dan were alone. She would be all too aware of him then. It was becoming harder and harder to suppress that awareness, as well as her longing for something more between them than joint guardianship of Patrick. Mornings were the worst, when they would meet at the coffee pot. His sleep-husky voice and tousled just-got-out-of-bed look made her yearn to drag him back—to her bed. That was bad, she acknowledged. Very bad.

"Now I understand that neither of you has ever had children," the reporter said. "How has it been suddenly having a baby to care for?"

Angelica smothered another sigh. Obviously, this woman wasn't any more imaginative than the other reporters. Every one so far had also used the angle of inexperienced couple suddenly in charge of a baby.

She fought the urge to say: "We've dropped him

four times, given him pizza and soda, and once accidentally threw him out with the bathwater." Nobody would appreciate the joke except Dan. They had their instructions, which helped tremendously, plus daily advice from Martha during her visits. They were feeling a little less helpless, and Patrick, thank goodness, was a happy-go-lucky baby. Either that, or he was being extremely patient.

To her amusement, Dan answered with what he called his short, sanitized version of the truth. "It's been hectic, but we've managed."

Patrick, who was posed between her and Dan, let out a scream of delight, waved his arms, then grabbed the heavy gold chain she was wearing and yanked it. The Star of the Show clearly wasn't about to let the attention drift far from him.

"Well, Patrick's been having fun," Dan quipped.

"Thanks," Angelica muttered, as he helped her disentangle her jewelry from Patrick's grasping fingers. She absently slung the chain behind her so it hung down her back out of reach and said to the baby, "You could get ten to twenty for that stuff, kid."

Everybody laughed, and the reporter looked inordinately pleased at capturing a spontaneous moment on film.

Angelica held her patience through the rest of the questions. It seemed especially ridiculous now to sit through them, knowing perhaps a minute of the interview would make it on the air. Patrick loved the fuss, she admitted, smiling indulgently as he grinned and "talked" for the camera. The interview wound down at last.

Almost.

"And now if you two would kiss for the camera."

"What!" she and Dan exclaimed in mutual astonishment.

"A kiss." The reporter chuckled, as she looked expectantly at them. "The people at home will love it, Angelica."

Angelica cleared her throat as her brain scrambled for a quick but acceptable excuse.

Dan laid his hand on her arm, drawing her attention. His gaze held amused annoyance at first, then she caught a fleeting glimpse of something else as he leaned forward. Before she could protest, his lips settled on hers gently, almost chastely . . . and for altogether too long. She felt as if she'd suddenly plunged into swirling rapids, and she sensed within Dan an intensity barely held back. He finally lifted his head and smiled benignly at her. Suddenly conscious of the camera, she tried not to gasp for breath. All the air seemed to have left her body.

"Well, that was terrific," the reporter said. "The entire interview was terrific. Thanks so much for doing it."

"You're welcome," Dan said, looking as unruffled as ever.

Angelica managed to pull herself together enough to nod her agreement.

It was another half-hour before the JBM-TV people finally left, and Angelica could ask the question that had been burning inside her for quite some time.

"Was that necessary?" she demanded as she laid Patrick on the changing table. It was set up in a corner of the sitting room they both now termed "the baby's room." She began to remove Patrick's "good" clothes.

"Was what necessary?" Dan asked as he handed her a diaper.

"Kissing for the camera."

"Why wouldn't an engaged couple kiss? You want pajamas or a playsuit?"

"Pajamas. I want to try to get him to nap." Dan set a pair on the end of the table as she returned to her original subject. "Dan, this is complicated enough without playing for the camera."

"It must have been a lousy kiss, since you're complaining."

"No—"

"Ahhh!" he interrupted, grinning. "Then it was a great kiss."

"No!" She set her jaw, resisting the urge to do him bodily harm. Instead, she struggled to get the squirming Patrick changed. Dan stood by and helped as needed. Since they had started doing things together, rather than fight over the privilege, it had become automatic to help each other with the baby. Dan's assistance mollified her slightly.

"I'm only saying we play games for the media alone, okay?"

"We'll see."

"Dan—" The telephone rang, and she swore silently. "That's probably Martha wanting to know how things went. You talk to her."

"That's cruel and inhuman punishment," Dan said.

"I know," she replied sweetly. "Answer the phone, Danny."

Grumbling, he went to answer the telephone. Angelica had Patrick ready by the time he returned. Without a word, he took the baby to give him his bottle.

"Martha is pleased," he announced, once he settled in a chair with Patrick. He gazed at Angelica for a long moment. "She's positive the wider coverage will bring someone forward about Patrick."

An odd weariness settled into Angelica's bones at the thought of progress made in Patrick's case. She knew he would leave when a good home was ready, but she was really starting to hate the thought of that happening.

Not wanting to talk about it, she sat down on the sofa and changed the subject to something else that had been bothering her lately. "You know, Dan, you don't need to take time off from your company like you have been. I can take care of Patrick by myself."

"I hope not in the same way you handled giving Patrick his bath the other day."

"It was only a little water," she said in her defense.

"About seven gallons worth, all over the bathroom floor."

"Well, you were no better warming his bottle."

"I never would have thought they could melt like that," he said musingly, then added, "It's only fair for me to pitch in, Angelica, and do my half. I can work out of the suite for a short time, too, like you're doing. Besides, you'd never let me hear the end of it if I left you all the dirty work. Barring diapers, of course."

"Of course," she muttered, feeling defeated. Where, she wondered, were the chauvinists when a person needed them?

Still, she had to get Dan out of the suite more, and running a company was an ideal reason. It irritated her for some reason to have him shouldering half of Patrick's care. She hadn't wanted to know that Dan was capable of such a commitment. She certainly didn't need a demonstration. And it was endearing to watch him with Patrick, and she didn't want to find him endearing, either. And their cooperation drove her crazy, simply because they were becoming easier, more comfortable with each other. She also had no idea how to define their living arrangement. Bizarre was probably an understatement. The implications, however, were cause for alarm, particularly when she considered the ache she felt every night when they went into their separate bedrooms, without even a friendly good-night kiss. Add to that the continual reannouncement of their "engagement" to the press, who in turn broadcast it up and down the West Coast.

Her growing attachment to Patrick was frightening enough, she thought. She'd seen how love could tear a person apart. In Patrick's case, she was braced for it. But she sensed that she'd lose a large part of herself if she ever fell in love with Dan. She couldn't allow that. And yet the whole problem was she had no control over the situation. She'd created a monster and was trapped by it.

"Don't forget we have to go to dinner at my parents' tonight," he said.

She groaned. But that at least was a subject she could argue and gladly.

"That's another thing, Dan," she began. "I really don't see any reason why *I* have to go to dinner at your parents'."

He eyed her for a long moment. "But you will go, Angelica."

It was the calm, extremely gentle tone that caught her attention. She swallowed back a sudden wariness and continued.

"I know your mother hasn't been too thrilled about all this publicity, but we are doing it at the department's request. To help get information—"

"We've accepted, and we're going to dinner tonight. Think of it as a first outing for Patrick." His voice was calmer than ever. "You won't like the consequences if you don't."

Angelica remembered Dan's coolly prim mother from her cousin's wedding. She also remembered Dan's anger when his mother had called after the first newspaper article. Okay, so she owed him one for accidentally causing so much havoc, but did it have to be this one? She really didn't want to face Natalie Roberts's unhappiness at the sudden change in her son's life-style. But barring that, she was very uneasy at the idea of "Dinner at Mom's." It was too much like a real family. Something they weren't.

"Angelica."

"Okay, okay. Dinner tonight at your parents'," she said, then added under her breath, "if I don't get the flu first."

Dan removed the bottle from Patrick's drowsy mouth. He got up and laid Patrick on his stomach in the crib, all the while crooning, "Ple-e-e-ase, Patrick, take a nap."

Angelica couldn't help giggling at his begging tone. Patrick only woke up once a night, which she'd been told was very good, but naps were rather hit-or-miss affairs. Of course, there had been no opportunity to begin a routine for him either. She was starting to worry, since Jan Williamson, the pediatrician, had stressed a baby's need for routine.

She watched Patrick stretch once and close his eyes, not fighting sleep. Her heart turned over at the sweetness of his expression, and she steeled herself against it. She was afraid to admit how much she was coming to care for Patrick.

Dan turned around and grinned at her. "You have just witnessed great talent at work," he whispered.

Angelica had to laugh. And that frightened her too. Damn, she thought. She felt as if she were being pulled in ten different directions, without an opportunity to deal properly with even one.

Knowing she was helpless against her fate for the moment, she put it from her mind and decided to take care with her appearance, tonight. It was a first outing of sorts for her too.

Anyway, if she couldn't cope, she could at least look good.

•   •   •

"Are you sure you want to wear that dress?"

Even as the question left his lips, Dan cursed the thought of Angelica changing from the sassy pale red dress into something more . . . something. The long-sleeved silk dress skimmed her slender body before it ended several inches above her knees. The swells of her breasts were generously visible above the low-cut heart-shaped neckline, although it wasn't a shocking exposure of creamy flesh. Maybe it was the eye-catching way the delicate diamond pendant of her necklace nestled between the delicious curves. There wasn't any one thing about the dress that would draw scandalized glances, but the overall effect was enough to raise a man's blood pressure.

"Yes, I'm sure I want to wear this dress." She gave him a puzzled look as she picked Patrick up. "Why? What's wrong with it?"

"Nothing," he said truthfully. Taking a deep calming breath, he admitted that the dress raised something all right. Enviously, he watched Patrick clutch her breasts with tiny innocent hands.

"Lucky son of a gun," he muttered. He'd seen the baby do that on more than one occasion, and had wondered if he'd ever get the chance to do the same. He sure as hell hoped so. Maintaining a platonic relationship with Angelica had been difficult enough before. Now that they were living together, he had to struggle constantly to keep his hands off her.

"Did you say something?" she asked.

"No."

"Dan, the dress is fine. I've worn it to dinners with clients. Even my mother likes this dress."

"Forget it," he said. "It's a great dress. I don't even know why I brought the subject up—"

"Yes, you do. You don't think it's appropriate to wear to dinner at your parents' house." She sighed. "And you're right. But all my clothes, if you'll remember, are in San Francisco. Besides, when have I had time to shop for jeans, let alone a dress?"

He shook his head and admitted freely and with relish that she drove him crazy. Everything about her was outwardly fresh and energetic and defiant. But there was more, much more to her than he'd ever imagined. The deep vulnerability she'd shown earlier tempered all of his reactions to her now. They still argued, yet there was a sense of zest rather than anger to it. The latest interview popped into his head, and he forced it away. He didn't want to think about their "engagement." It left him helplessly angry at the way it had ballooned into the media story of the year. And yet he found himself more drawn to her now that they were "engaged." The only thing he didn't feel confused or frustrated about was their original reason for doing it—Patrick. And because of that, he held his patience on all the rest.

"Got everything?" he asked, knowing they should be going.

She glanced around, ticking off her list out loud. "Bag with diapers, bottles, change of clothes, pajamas, extra formula, extra wipes; toys, in case he gets bored; rocker chair, so he can sit or sleep; carseat. Is there anything else we should take, do you think?"

"The question is," he asked in disbelief, "is there anything else *left*?"

"Not much," she replied, chuckling.

"I feel like we're moving in," he said, beginning to gather up all the gear.

"Don't worry, Danny." She patted his cheek as she swept by to the door. "I'll probably get us kicked out again with this dress."

No doubt of that, he thought as he considered his mother's reaction to Angelica. His father, a jovial, easygoing man, would love her. But his mother was a little more . . rigid. She had not been happy about his suddenly acquiring a "fiancée" and a baby, however temporarily. He couldn't help feeling worried about the evening ahead.

Once they were in the parking garage under the hotel, he packed everything but the carseat in the trunk of his Mercedes sports coupe. The carseat, sans Patrick for the moment, he knew could only go into the stowage space behind the two bucket seats.

He crawled into the car and set the seat in the back. Or tried to.

"Damn," he muttered, attempting to jam the seat into the long narrow space. He was forced to lean over the seats at an awkward angle, and he couldn't really get leverage. The infant seat sank several inches, but at a tilt, before it stubbornly refused to move farther.

"What's the matter?" Angelica called from the open car door.

"The seat won't go in."

"But it has to!" she exclaimed. "It isn't safe for Patrick to sit on my lap."

"I know that!"

He lifted the carseat out, and keeping it level, tried again. It didn't work. He stopped and studied it for several minutes, then tried once more. He pushed, shoved, and rocked the carseat every way possible, but the damn thing would not go into the stowage space. Finally, exasperated and panting for breath, he climbed out of the car and stared at Angelica. He knew what the alternative was, and he dreaded it.

"Well?" she prompted.

"It won't fit in the back, so it has to go on the passenger seat."

"The passenger seat! But where will I sit?"

He cleared his throat, then took the baby out of her arms. Puzzled, she let Patrick go. He unashamedly admitted to holding the baby for added protection. Surely, she wouldn't hit a man with an infant.

"Well, you'll . . . ah, have to exchange places with Patrick."

Her eyes widened in shock and horror as realization dawned. "No! I cannot sit back there!"

"It will be a little cramped, but you're thin enough to squeeze into it," he said in a rush, hoping to persuade her.

"I'm not squeezing anywhere!" She scrambled into the car and began her own efforts to get the carseat into the back. . . .

When Dan finally drove the Mercedes out of the parking garage, he tried not to listen to the occupant of the passenger seat coo and gurgle at the bright lights flashing by the car's windshield. It wouldn't really be fair to enjoy Patrick's new adventure, he told himself. Not when Angelica was making such a tremendous sacrifice. A snort of amusement escaped him, despite his best efforts.

"Daniel Roberts, are you laughing?" Angelica demanded in forbidding tones from behind him.

"I'm honestly trying not to," he said, unsuccessfully smothering his amusement.

"That does not appease me."

"I'm sorry," he said, meaning it. He really did feel bad that she was stuck in the back. The problem was he just couldn't properly express it at the moment. "Consider it my revenge for our 'engagement'."

"Is it?"

"No, but maybe you'll feel better."

She was silent for a moment, then said, "I'm renting a car with four seats and four doors first thing tomorrow. And I'm charging it to you."

"You drive a hard bargain."

"You drive a useless car."

He laughed.

Dan found himself smiling broadly as he drove toward his parents' home in Issaquah. This really was the first time he and Angelica had had an opportunity just to talk or tease each other. The car insured that no Canfield or hotel people or Starlight executives or clients could interrupt them. Or parents demanding attendance at dinner, either. Even Patrick was temporarily immobilized by the carseat, and clearly happy as a clam to go "bye-bye."

He hadn't realized the tremendous number of demands they'd both been coping with since discovering the child. And they had coped with them together. Even now, Angelica faced the stowage space with grace.

He remembered how he had thought they *couldn't* have a relationship. It would be very interesting to find out if he were wrong.

As Angelica fatalistically watched Patrick spit up on the shoulder of her silk dress, she finally admitted this was not her evening.

"You probably fed him too much," Dan's mother said reprovingly.

Angelica gritted her teeth as she dipped a corner of her napkin in her water glass. She swiped at the spot with one hand while trying not to bump Patrick's nose. Smiling back her temper, she said politely, "He was very hungry, though, wasn't he?"

"You really have to be careful not to overfeed—"

"Mom," Dan interrupted as he took Patrick from Angelica. He looked so angry that she smiled at him to show him she was trying to be tolerant. He turned to his mother and said, "Could Angelica have a wet towel or something for her dress?"

"Oh! Of course," his mother replied, looking surprised at the question. She immediately bustled out of the dining room and Angelica resisted the urge to sigh in momentary respite.

With her hands now free, she worked desperately at the stain while she silently cursed her fate. First she'd had to sit in that vise of a stowage space. That she'd come out of it with only a frazzled composure, a numb fanny, and two small runs in her hose was a miracle. The welcome from Dan's mother had been decidedly cool, and Mrs. Roberts had shown her further disapproval by constantly correcting Angelica's baby care techniques. The overfeeding was only the last of a long list, and it shook what little confidence she'd acquired in handling a baby.

And now this, Angelica thought in disgust. She'd had experience with this stuff before and knew the odor would linger forever. 'Eau de spit-up' had staying power.

Harvey Roberts, Dan's father, cleared his throat. "Well, now, this little charmer has caused quite a ruckus, hasn't he?"

Angelica stifled a giggle. Poor man, she thought. He had repeated that phrase at least six times so far to break a tense silence. She liked him immensely.

It was so obvious that both of Dan's parents were thrown by what had happened that she really shouldn't, and couldn't, blame them for their bewilderment and slight antagonism. The best she could do under the circumstances was hold her temper and pray for a very quick end to the evening.

Natalie Roberts came back into the room and handed Angelica a wet dish towel. "I mixed in a little lemon juice to help remove any staining or odor."

Surprised by the gesture, Angelica smiled warmly at the older woman. "Thank you very much."

"Lemon juice?" Dan asked.

His mother nodded. "I found it helpful when you were a baby."

"What your mother means is you were the greatest—"

"Harvey!"

"Well, you were a messy kid," Harvey finished cryptically.

Angelica giggled out loud this time.

Dan groaned. He adjusted his glasses and said, "Please, Dad. Don't tell Angelica any more. She'll use it for ammunition."

"Me!" Angelica exclaimed innocently. "Never. Anyway, you were probably a good baby."

"Don't bet on it," Harvey said, warming to the subject. "Natalie always said that if Dan had come first, there would have been no second."

"Really?" Angelica asked, turning to Dan's mother. They all did, their grins wide with anticipation.

Natalie blushed red.

"He was a terror, Nat, wasn't he?" Harvey said, chuckling.

To Angelica's surprise, Natalie gazed fondly at her husband and Dan. "Yes, he was." Then she instantly straightened and the moment was gone. Still it served to break the ice a little, and the rest of the evening went somewhat more smoothly.

When they finally pulled out of the Roberts's driveway, Dan said, "I'm sorry, Angelica. My mother was very close to being rude several times."

"Don't be sorry," she said, feeling badly for him. "I was just realizing tonight how this must affect them."

"You didn't twist my arm about all this, you know."

"Don't argue with me when I'm trying to be generous," she said reprovingly. "Besides, I don't think my parents would have been any better."

He chuckled. "Thanks for putting up with mine."

She glanced over the seat at Patrick, who already had his eyes closed. "He certainly knows how to cause a stir."

"I think my father already said that," Dan commented in an innocent voice.

Angelica laughed.

They no sooner got off the elevator, when they spotted Martha Canfield waiting impatiently for them.

Despite her bulk, she hurried toward them. "Where the hell have you been?"

"Out to dinner," Dan said.

"Out to dinner!" Martha glared at them. "You weren't in the hotel restaurant. I checked."

"We were at Dan's parents' in Issaquah,' Angelica said helpfully.

Martha gasped. "Issaquah!"

Seeing Patrick stir slightly from his pillow of feminine shoulder, Dan set his jaw. This was getting ridiculous, he thought. Everyone was demanding time and explanations, and he was tired of it. All they had done was go to dinner, and dammit, they didn't have to check in with Martha before they did.

He brushed past the big woman without answering. At the entrance to the suite he set down the baby paraphernalia he was carrying and unlocked the door. When it opened, he put his hand at Angelica's waist and urged her over the threshold. "Why don't you go in, Angelica, and get Patrick into bed? I'll straighten this out."

She gazed at him, a smile hovering about her lips "Fine."

"Now," he said, as he pulled the door closed behind her, "what is the problem, Martha?"

"The problem was that I called and received no answer, so I came over to find that you weren't here." She seemed to enlarge in her fury. "I checked with the front desk, and no one knew where the two of you had gone!"

"Are you saying that we can't take Patrick out of this suite without your permission?" Dan demanded.

"I need to know where he is at all times!" Martha said in righteous indignation.

"Do you require that of all your other temporary guardians?"

The big woman looked nonplussed for a moment. "Well, no. But you two are a special case."

"And I'm getting tired of us being a special case. You visit every day to make sure we haven't damaged the poor kid, and when you're not here, you're calling. And then there's the press. Angelica and I have obliged in every instance without complaint, and yet we are treated like three-year-olds."

"Look—"

"I know you're concerned, but all this will stop now, Martha. No more daily visits, no more phone calls every half-hour, no more press interviews. It's very disruptive to Patrick, and exhausting for Angelica. We'll work out a more reasonable arrangement."

"I realize that it hasn't been easy for you two, and you know I'm grateful to you both for being willing to take on the responsibility of a baby." Martha smiled slightly. "But I took a real chance on both of you, and I have to make sure it was the right choice. I have to know where he is."

Dan came to an instant decision. He knew exactly how he could protect his temporary family, and get to know Angelica better at the same time.

"Fine. You have to know where he is, then I'll be glad to tell you. Starting tomorrow. Patrick will be at my home on Nadera Island."

Five

Angelica gazed around the oak and glass living room, listened to the silence, and sighed.

"How did you ever manage it?"

Dan smiled smugly. "I keep telling you. Talent."

She was dubious. "No more press interviews?"

"You don't even have to look at a newspaper."

"No inspection by Martha?"

"Not even a peek."

"No phone call from her every two seconds?"

"Well, one in the morning, and one in the evening." He grinned lopsidedly. "I couldn't quite get around that."

"Ya done good," she drawled.

"Thank you. The only drawback to this place is no room service. However, the freezer is stocked, and we can get whatever else we need from the general store in the village."

She gasped dramatically. "What! You mean we'll have to cook! Not quite as cocky as you think, are you?"

His grin widened. "Try me."

"What a beautiful view," she exclaimed, looking out the floor-to-ceiling glass doors that opened onto a redwood patio and faced the white-capped Straits of Juan de Fuca. It was beautiful. Although she knew there were other houses and even a small village on the island, she could see only pine trees and water. The fabulous view lifted her sagging spirits and she realized just how tired she was. She had been given breathing space, and she planned to push all her worries from her mind and enjoy it.

"You know what I want to do first?" she said, turning back around.

"Sleep."

"You too?"

"I'm looking forward to finding the nearest bed and sacking out." He began to unfold the playpen. "When I'm finally done setting up everything for Patrick. Are you sure we needed all this?"

She sighed. "We had this argument before we left. It's just his playpen and stroller, some clothes, bottles, and diapers. It only looks like a lot."

"It was four trips to that big rental car of yours to get it all in."

"Better than forgetting something important."

"We live in fear of that, don't we? I think I'll have duplicates of everything sent here for next time."

She grinned at him, then changed the subject. She didn't like thinking there might not be a "next time." "Maybe I can finally get some work done." Her secretary had sent up all the files and papers she needed, and yet Angelica had barely glanced through them. "I still can't believe we'll all be like normal kids and adults. I feel now as if I could breeze through only Patrick and work."

"I know." Dan paused in setting up the playpen. "I'm hoping to catch up on my paperwork at least."

"Thank you," she said solemnly, "for giving Martha hell."

"You're welcome." He laughed. "Actually, I enjoyed it. Kind of felt like standing up to Sister Agnes."

"Who's Sister Agnes?"

"The Dragon Lady of my youth." He shrugged, looking a little like a shy young boy trying to be nonchalant. "All of this has been rough on you, and you've been wonderful, Angelica."

She shrugged as nonchalantly as possible in return and walked over to the sofa. The carseat, Patrick still strapped into it, was sitting on one of the cushions. She began to undo the buckles, and the baby grinned at her. She smiled back.

"It wasn't so bad," she finally said to Dan. "Anyway, it's hard to say no to something for Patrick."

"I like him, too. Stick him in here until everything's unpacked." Dan stood up. He tossed in his keys, and they bounced once with a jingle on the playpen mat. Patrick's head shot up and he gurgled happily.

"I know at least three people who would tell you those are unsanitary for Patrick to play with," Angelica said, lifting the baby into her arms.

Dan's expression was innocent. "I'm contributing to his immune system. The more germs he comes into contact with, the more natural immunizations his body will create. Therefore, fewer allergies and less illness."

"You're a wonderful humanitarian."

"Thank you. Just don't tell the Nobel Prize people that it's the big round medallion on the key chain and the noise the keys make that he likes."

She set Patrick into the playpen and watched as he reached for the keys. "You're sure there's a doctor on the island?"

"Yes, Angelica. He's retired, but always available. And if anything serious happens, we can have Patrick back in Seattle very quickly. Quit worrying."

"I'm not worried. A little anxious, but not worried."

She moved away from the playpen. Getting away to Dan's home on the island had its advantages, but there was one other *little* thing that was niggling at her. She decided to broach it subtly.

"Well," she said, clapping her hands together, "where do you want Patrick's and my things?"

Dan gave her an indecipherable look. "There are several rooms upstairs you can choose from."

"Fine."

She gathered up as much as she could carry, while Dan toted the portable crib he'd rented in Seattle. As she followed him upstairs, she found herself assessing the way his olive-green shirt clung to his strong shoulders. His jeans, faded and comfortable-looking, drew the eye to narrow hips and long legs. There was something about him that spelled confidence . . . and experience. It was rather like seeing the Superman in Clark Kent—unexpected and very intriguing.

A small, sensible voice inside her reminded her she couldn't afford to be intrigued.

"This is a beautiful house," she said, forcing her gaze from his backside. Talking would cover her nervousness. She hoped. "It reminds me a little of Diana's."

"We computer programmers have great taste."

Dan, she knew, had been a programmer like her cousin before deciding to start his own software company.

"I hate to tell you this, Dan, but you aren't a programmer anymore."

"There are times when I regret that."

The words surprised her. She never would have thought Dan was bothered by leaving the programming behind. "You can always hire someone to run the company, you know, and go back to it."

"I'd still have the ultimate responsibility. Unless I sold Starlight."

She gasped. "Dan, you aren't thinking of that?"

"No, I'm not." He gave her a quick grin over his shoulder. "While I miss the programming, the truth is, I do like owning my own company better. Most of the time. What, did I scare you?"

"Of course," she said caustically. "Think of the horrendous amount of paperwork I'd have to do for Diana's part in Starlight."

He chuckled.

Upstairs, Angelica walked almost cautiously down

the hall, anxious about what he might suggest for room arrangements. Finally he indicated one room as "nursery" and the door opposite for her.

She glanced briefly inside her room and was vastly relieved to see what was obviously a guest room.

"This looks great," she said enthusiastically, stepping over the threshold.

"I thought you'd like it."

Something in his tone made her turn around. His gaze flicked over her, and a slight smile hovered about his mouth. She had the distinct impression he had been aware of her nervousness. And liked it.

She swallowed.

Maybe things weren't going to be quite as relaxing as she'd thought.

"It's a bird. It's a plane. It's SuperPatrick!"

Holding Patrick in his arms, Dan carefully raced around the patio. The baby grinned sloppily in his delight.

"This beats the heck out of working, doesn't it," he said to Patrick. "Now all we have to do is persuade Angelica of that."

"I'm combining work and relaxation," she said, from her seat on the chaise longue. Papers, weighted down by pens, cups, soda cans, and even rocks, were strewn on a small table and the foot of the lounger. "You ought to try it, Danny. SuperPatrick could probably use a break."

There was the nickname again, Dan thought with satisfaction. She'd been using it more and more since they had arrived at the island three days ago. Every time he heard it, something very primitive ran through his veins. Seeing her dressed in her new jeans, oversized red shirt, and cheap plastic thongs only strengthened his basic reaction. She could wear anything and look completely and totally sexy.

"Let him be SuperPatrick a little longer," he said. "He's going to have to take a nap soon anyway."

She shook her head and chuckled. "You mean you're having too much fun."

"That too. What do you think about letting him take a nap out here on the patio?"

"Only if you promise to work."

"Angelica, you're turning into a nag."

"I'm protecting Patrick," she said solemnly. "You'd be picking him up the first time he rolled over, so you could play again. You've done it before. Honestly, the poor kid wouldn't get any sleep if you had your way."

"Thanks," he grumbled. But he sat down in one of the patio chairs, just in case she was right and he was playing too much with the baby. "He's a good kid, though, isn't he?"

She lifted her head and smiled affectionately at Patrick. "Yes. My secretary Jane says that some babies are just happy babies, easygoing. Patrick certainly seems that way."

Dan looked horrified. "You mean this could be worse?"

She shrugged. "He's a lot of work, but he's not crying all the time."

"Except when he's hungry. Then he turns into a screaming machine."

"Well, he can't be perfect. But Lord knows, he's patient with us about everything else."

"Sssshhh!" Dan hissed. "He might catch on that we're idiots about babies."

She laughed. "I think he already knows."

He realized that this was one of the easiest conversations the two of them had ever had. Coming to his island home was probably the best idea he'd had since forming Starlight Software. The longer they stayed isolated like this, the more she would lose her wariness of him.

If he could hold out, he admitted to himself. Angelica was intoxicating, and he deliberately refrained from touching her. He sensed that part of her stiffness with him was because of their personality differences in the past, although that, thanks to Patrick, was easing. But there was more to it. In odd moments, he recognized that she was vulnerable and afraid. He wanted her, yet he knew she could not be pressed. She would freeze up and bolt.

It would have to start in friendship, he thought. And Patrick was the key. Angelica had begun to view him with something other than dislike. And he had begun to see exactly the kind of woman she was—fierce and fragile, serene and determined. Fire and ice that had obsessed him from the beginning.

"Dan."

Her low, enticing voice broke the spell of his thoughts.

"What?" he asked, glancing over at her.

She pointed to the baby in his arms. "I think your buddy has had enough."

He looked down to see Patrick sound asleep against his chest.

"It's probably the air," he said, carefully standing up with his burden.

"Probably."

Angelica's smile held an odd intimacy, and Dan felt as if someone had punched him in the stomach.

She might eventually lose her stiffness with him, he thought, but he had the feeling he'd turn to stone.

"Okay, so we needed the stroller."

Angelica smothered a grin at Dan's grumpy tone, as he pushed the umbrella stroller up the dirt road toward the house hidden behind the trees. Glancing sideways, she could discern his grimace of surrender in the deepening twilight.

"You could always have carried Patrick," she said.

"Point of order, counselor. I've conceded already."

She laughed. "Point taken. By the way, Nadera is a nice place."

They had decided to take a walk through Nadera's tiny "one-horse" village after dinner. One horse was about all there was room for, Angelica thought. There was a cluster of clapboard houses around a small central green containing one flagpole. Add a general store in the back of the Stein house, and that was it.

"I like it," Dan said. "And Patrick liked the fuss everyone made over him."

"He's a celebrity, and the little ham knows it. Who was that old man who kept tweaking Patrick's nose?"

"Old Mr. Stein, as opposed to his son who is *not* known as young Mr. Stein, just Asa."

"Ah. Well, Patrick loved him."

"I think Patrick likes it here too." He leaned down to look at the baby. "Don't you, buddy?"

Patrick was busy gazing upward at the dark, looming tree branches. It was hard to tell exactly what he was thinking, but Dan smiled triumphantly anyway.

Dammit, Angelica thought, as she forced herself to smile back. For the past week she'd continually had to be careful not to be drawn into her own lie, yet it was increasingly harder to resist Dan. He didn't have to make her laugh, too.

Later, after Patrick was settled in his crib, she pulled on a sweater and stepped out onto the patio. Clouds drifted across a quarter moon, and the ceaseless sound of surf washing along the shoreline reached her ears. Although the patio was lit, the forest loomed darkly just feet away. The scene should have soothed her, should have eased her inner tensions. Somehow, though, it brought back her earlier thoughts of Dan more sharply.

She could feel the restlessness of her body, the long denial of femininity slowly crumbling. It was the damn closeness to Dan, she decided. She tried to relax her tense muscles, telling herself she was only reacting to the situation. She would have felt the same way with any attractive man.

If only she were promiscuous, she thought half-seriously. She wouldn't be suffering now for suppressing the birds and the bees. Hell, she wouldn't have any emotional conflicts, either.

The patio doors slid open behind her, and she whirled around in time to see Dan step outside.

"Nice evening," he said, and took a deep breath.

She could almost feel his chest expand with air. The muscles were stretching under his shirt and his rib cage was lifting. . . .

She swallowed and croaked out, "Yes, it is a nice evening. Is Patrick asleep?"

He nodded. "I assume so. I didn't hear anything."

"Maybe that room is too far away," she began, "and with the door closed . . . I better go in."

"I didn't mean to chase you inside. Stay a few minutes more and enjoy it. Even if Patrick does wake up, he'll be fine for a while."

She had no excuse to get around his sensible logic. That was the problem with former computer programmers, she thought with irritation. They knew their logic.

"You know," he continued, "this past week has taught me to deeply appreciate moments like this." He walked over to the edge of the patio, near to where she hovered by the wall. "The silence, the serenity, the . . ."

". . . nothing to do," she finished.

He chuckled. "That, too."

He had said only a few minutes, and she knew she couldn't leave yet without looking silly. She might be a little sex-starved, but she was, she hoped, mature.

"It seems strange," she said, praying she sounded neutrally pleasant, "that just a short time ago, I was in an intricate business meeting, fighting for my client's rights. And now my biggest fight is how to get a sleeper suit on Patrick while he's trying to roll onto his stomach. I did better with what's-his-face from Mark IV Computers."

"Mitch Garner."

"Right. What's-his-face. By the way, have you heard anything from them?"

"Oh." His abashed grin was easy to see in the patio lighting. "I meant to tell you I got a message that they've asked for another meeting."

"Oh, Lord," she muttered. "How can I hold a meeting with Patrick? I don't know if I can."

"Before you panic, you might want to know that *I* panicked. I told Clark to tell Mark IV we'd get back to them."

She immediately relaxed. "Thank goodness."

She lifted her face to the night, and breathed in the crisp air one last time. . . .

Dan started to laugh. She lowered her chin and asked, "What's so funny?"

"You. There was a time when you would have pounced on me about that phone call. In fact, you would have given me hell for not telling you about it."

Her eyes widened, and she stared at him in astonishment. "I didn't, did I? It seems . . . unimportant . . . while Patrick is so clearly important."

"It's funny how a little guy like him can just take over your life, isn't it?"

"Astounding," she agreed. "And you don't even know it. Do you remember that first night? I was so terrified that he'd break."

"I was terrified there'd be more diapers like that first one."

"There have been."

"You mean I've grown accustomed to it?"

She giggled. "Somebody has to. I never thought, though, that I would be so . . . selfless."

"Angelica, you've always been unselfish—"

"No." She stepped over to the edge of the patio and stared into the blackness of the forest underbrush. "Not unselfish, although I thank you for the thought. Selfless. It's as if all the essentials are put on hold for someone else's sake. A little baby's. And it just seems so natural to do that."

His silence startled her, and she glanced over at him, wondering if she'd said anything that had offended him. He was staring at her fixedly, and she felt like a rabbit caught in an eagle's hungry gaze.

"You surprise me, Angelica," he said in a low voice. "Continually and unexpectedly, you surprise me."

She gaped at him, his words leaving her speechless.

He reached out and touched her cheek. "I promised myself I wouldn't do this. Not yet."

His fingers traced her jawline, lingering on her sensitive skin. His touch was mesmerizing her into a frozen statue. Despite the protest clamoring on the edge of her brain, she couldn't move or speak.

"I knew you would feel like cool porcelain," he said softly. "Now let me taste the fire."

He lowered his head.

Six

Dan felt her initial jolt of surprise, and he knew he
was rushing her. He had to back away, otherwise
he'd frighten her off. . . .

But he could feel the tips of her breasts brushing
his chest, her hands gripping his shoulders for balance. He needed just one more moment of bliss.

A low moan from the back of her throat reached
his ears, and then to his delighted astonishment,
her arms were winding around his neck, clinging
tightly as her lips moved against his.

He wanted her with a shocking fierceness, and he
gathered her closer. He plied her mouth with a quickening rhythm, feeling her respond with each change
and movement. Their tongues entwined, and he
tasted more than fire. He tasted a need that matched
his own.

His hands slipped of their own accord down her

back, his fingers trailing across the soft skin beneath her sweater. He cupped her derriere and pressed himself into her.

He had denied himself of her too long, he thought. He wanted her, needed her now, and damn the consequences. Her mouth was fast to his, and her arms were tight around his neck. She wanted him, he knew, and he wondered if all their arguing and disagreeing was a defense against their wild hunger for each other.

It would be so easy, he thought. And so wrong.

Cursing the sudden appearance of common sense, he forced himself to lift his head and set her away.

He cursed even more when he saw Angelica blink in confusion and gradually open her eyes. Her expression changed rapidly from lassitude to bewilderment to angry hurt.

"Well," he said, hoping to ease the tense silence, "we *are* engaged."

Her mouth lifted for an instant, then she schooled her expression. "I better go inside in case Patrick needs something."

She seemed so distant that he immediately said, "Angelica, let's discuss—"

"Dan, there's nothing to discuss," she said flatly. "We've been taking care of a baby together, and we just got caught up in 'playing house'."

He shook his head. "There's more to it than that, and I think you know it."

She looked away for an instant, then said, "I'm attracted, and I admit that. But it doesn't mean that there's any more. We've known each other for nearly a year. Don't you think if there were more between us, we would have acted on it before?"

"Maybe we've had obstacles."

"I doubt that would matter."

"Maybe we allowed them to matter."

She waved a hand. "You see? We can't even agree on why we kissed each other. Right now, we're making an effort to get along for Patrick's sake. We're not really being our normal selves. We reacted to the close quarters we've been sharing, and the constant togetherness. And that's all we did."

She turned around and strode into the house. Dan watched her go, grinning.

She had been fighting to deny the kiss. It was a reaction he understood and knew from her. Still, Angelica was not a woman to be pushed. What he had to do now was feed what the kiss had started.

He had a feeling he was going to enjoy that immensely.

Angelica tossed and turned in the guest bed, while listening to the patter of rain against the roof.

Damn, she thought, as she hopelessly tried yet again to wipe Dan's kiss from her mind. How could she have clung so desperately to him? How could she have fused her mouth to his like that? How could she have wanted it to go on forever?

It had been those stupid thoughts of being wanton that had caused her to react so . . . enthusiastically to him. In fact, she'd been past enthusiasm and heading into "unbridled passion" territory.

And knowing he was just yards away for yet another night made her want to get up and go to him.

It had just been an eruption of nature caused by their close proximity, she told herself firmly. Men didn't understand the intricacies of making love. They saw sex as a simple, straightforward function. But women lost a part of themselves, even in a simple, straightforward affair. At least she had. This time, though, was hardly simple or straightforward. She knew she would be the one who would be hurt afterward, when Patrick went to a permanent home and the affair between the adults came to an end. So why start something that was doomed in the first place?

She refused to step in with her eyes open and be knowingly hurt, and, dammit, being involved meant being hurt. That was insanity. This crazy situation demanded intimacy, nurtured the idea of union. Only the three of them weren't a union. They were an extremely temporary arrangement.

But she liked having the companionship of a man and the innocent love of a baby. Lord, but she liked it, she thought, swallowing back sudden tears. She believed she had been bracing herself for the inevitable. But, here, in the deep hours of the night, she finally admitted she hated the thought of giving up Patrick. She had tried to keep herself from feeling anything more than affection for the infant. But he was so helpless and so trusting that he was wrapping himself around her heart. Every smile, every chuckle, and even every fussy cry only added to her dilemma. Each day she had to keep telling herself that she was making sure he got the best, and when the best came along, she could and would let him go. There wasn't anything else she could do.

This should have been a night when she could have caught up on her sleep, she thought unhappily. Instead, it looked to be the longest of all.

"So what do you say, Patrick? Next time we come to the island, we'll bring poles and try a little surf fishing."

Smiling indulgently at Dan and Patrick, Angelica listened to the conversation as she sat on a rock and watched the waves pound against the beach. The Northwest waters were not kind, she thought, but they still allowed enough beach for a morning walk.

Pushing her windblown hair back from her cheek, she decided she felt much better. The morning had brought a renewed determination to stop worrying and just enjoy herself for the next few days. Surely, she was capable of that. All she had to do was make it clear to Dan that she'd meant what she'd said last night. So far, unfortunately, she hadn't found a proper moment to do so without spoiling things.

"I thought we came out for a walk," she said, getting up and dusting haphazardly at the damp sand clinging to her jeans.

"You're the one who stopped to sit on a rock," Dan said, from ten paces away. He was carrying Patrick since the stroller was practically useless on sand.

"So now I'm walking." She frowned as Patrick ducked his head away from the strong breeze. "I think it's a little too windy down here for the baby."

"Mmm." Dan pointed toward the trees. "There's a path that way that goes through the woods. What say we go look at the trees, buddy?"

Patrick sneezed.

"I hope he's not catching a cold," she muttered, staring speculatively at the baby.

"I hope not, too. How do we know if he's getting a cold?"

"He sneezes?" she asked, while inwardly cursing her ignorance. Patrick looked clear-eyed, dry-nosed, and normal. "Brother, you get a little confidence and bingo! The kid does something to throw you."

Dan chuckled. "Maybe it was just a sneeze. We all sneeze without having colds."

"True. I suppose we shouldn't panic before we have to." She looked at her watch. "We can walk in the woods as long as we don't dawdle. It's almost ten-thirty, time for Patrick's nap."

"Why do I feel you're going to be a drill sergeant about naps?" Dan asked, frowning.

"Because Patrick needs a routine. You know Jan said that."

"But he hasn't had one yet, and he's been fairly content."

"Dan," she said patiently, "all babies need a routine. It even says so in the baby book."

"That's right, it does."

Since she'd made progress with one subject, she decided to try a more intimate one.

"About last night," she began.

"Yes," he broke in. "I wanted to talk to you about that too. I think you were right."

"You do?" she asked in astonishment, instantly forgetting about sneezes and colds and naps and routines.

He nodded. "I was getting caught up in playing house with you. Okay, so we're attracted, but so what?"

She gasped. "So what!"

"Sure. Letting our attraction get out of control would be extremely foolish. After all, we both know how incompatible we are. Whatever attraction we feel is just momentary, and we can avoid blowing it out of proportion—"

"Out of proportion!"

"Right. We've got enough to do without our normal basic sexual urges complicating matters. We'd probably argue about it the same as we argue about everything else. I just want you to know that I am a man, but I can easily ignore that." He smiled kindly at her. "It won't be a problem again, I promise you."

"I see." A perverse anger shot through her at his vow. "Well, that's just wonderful, Dan. Just terrific. I think I'll go back to the house now. I'll take the road, it's shorter."

"Don't you want to walk through the woods?" he asked, surprised. "I promised Patrick we'd walk back that way."

"You go ahead." She waved a hand vaguely in the direction of the trees and started off toward the road.

As she strode quickly back to the house, she furiously decided to skewer one Daniel Roberts. Granted, she had wanted reassurances from him that the kiss wouldn't be repeated. But she definitely hadn't wanted to know that it would take *little* effort for him to restrain himself. And did he have to go on and on about their incompatibility? Once had been quite enough, she thought angrily.

Her feminine ego had taken a beating, and it was tempting to show him just how much effort it would take to keep from "complicating matters."

Very tempting.

Dan watched Angelica march up the beach and disappear over the small rising dunes.

"There's more than one way to avoid an argument, Patrick, my boy," he said with satisfaction.

Patrick grinned at him in infant innocence.

As he carefully walked through the gripping sand toward the edge of the woods, Dan admitted that outwitting Angelica was extremely stimulating. He wondered why he hadn't thought of it before.

"So much for a 180 IQ," he said to his companion. "I really am an idiot."

Last night he had thoroughly cursed his solitary bed. Then he'd decided it would be the last time. He had also realized how torn he'd been lately about Angelica. Despite his fascination with her, despite his longing to share his bed with her, his common sense told him it was foolish to pursue a relationship with someone as volatile as she. It would be a mistake to become involved with her. But last night he'd finally realized the truth.

Angelica was *not* a mistake.

She was unique, and she stirred things in him that no other woman had. Although he had put up a tremendous fight, he had never been able to ignore her. Maybe he'd sensed from the beginning that he wouldn't walk away from Angelica unscathed, and he hadn't been willing to risk himself until Patrick had come into his life and showed him just how sterile an existence he'd been living. He was risking, and gladly, his emotional well-being with the baby. It was impossible not to fall for Patrick, even knowing that the child would be leaving eventually. The old saying about it being better to have loved and lost than to have never loved at all suddenly made sense. He intended to "seize the day," as the Romans had. What the hell, he thought. If it was good enough for those centurions to conquer the Western World, then it was good enough for conquering Angelica.

Dan felt the baby clutch at the pocket of his jacket, and he glanced down and smiled as Patrick's head bobbed rhythmically with each step he took.

"I hope you don't get seasick," he said. "It would be a hell of a way to repay you for opening my eyes."

Once he had faced his fate last night, the problem had been to bring fate around to thinking the same way he did. Persuading Angelica would not be easy. He had racked his brains for a way to woo her, then realized that he had years of logic training at his command. Logic was action and reaction. All he had to do was find the right action to produce the right reaction in Angelica. It had hit him that if he acted as if the kiss had meant nothing, she would probably *react* in the opposite way. She was used to disagreeing with him, after all. It certainly looked as if his method of wooing her was off to a beautiful start.

"A little application of logic, Patrick, and you too can have that pretty girl in the next playpen panting to play with your blocks."

Then he added, "We hope."

"Yes, Martha, he's just fine and dandy," Angelica said into the telephone receiver. "In fact, he's been in bed for close to an hour."

"I'm glad to hear it," Martha said. "You sound less harried, Angelica."

"I feel less harried," she admitted, as she sat at the kitchen table and absently fiddled with the curled cord of the telephone. Talking to Martha was a release from thinking about the non-argument argument she'd had with Dan on the beach that morning. She'd had plenty of time to think about it too. When Patrick went down for his morning nap, Dan had finally decided to tackle his paperwork. He had briefly appeared for lunch and had played with Patrick, then had gone back to work, once again leaving her alone. Maybe if she kept talking she'd get it out of her mind once and for all, she thought. "And coming to the island has been good for Patrick too, Martha. We're getting into a routine."

"Excellent. I'm less worried about letting you go, although please don't take him into Victoria. Since that's Canada, it could cause all sorts of complications if anything should happen."

Angelica chuckled, envisioning Martha's panic if

they unthinkingly went shopping in Victoria. "You sound a little like you expect us to vanish across the border with the treasure."

"My boss would have my head on a pike if you did."

"And then you would have ours."

"You got it."

Angelica grinned at Martha's stern tone. "I promise we'll exercise our right to stay in this country. Have you . . ." She swallowed back a lump of anxiety. "Have you made any progress on Patrick?"

There was a slight hesitation before Martha said, "No, no one's showed up or given us any information on him. We did a national check using his footprint, and it looks like his birth wasn't registered."

Angelica gasped. "But that's impossible! Everyone has a birth certificate. The hospitals do it automatically."

"Not every baby is born in a hospital," Martha said. "In fact, the numbers that aren't would shock you. From the beginning, I've felt that Patrick's mother is probably an unwed teenager from a depressed background . . . or a runaway, and scared to come forward now that she's abandoned him. We'll find something eventually; we usually do. But it will take a while."

"What about . . ." Angelica drew in a deep breath. "What about a permanent home for him?"

"I hope to have something on that very soon. You two have been great, but I know how disruptive this has been to your lives. Believe me, the department's working hard on this—"

America's most popular, most compelling romance novels...

Here, at last...love stories that really involve you! Fresh, finely crafted novels with story lines so believable you'll feel you're actually living them! Characters you can relate to...exciting places to visit...unexpected plot twists...all in all, exciting romances that satisfy your mind and delight your heart.

Get one full-length Loveswept FREE every month!
Now you can be sure you'll never, ever miss a single
Loveswept title by enrolling in our special reader's home
delivery service. A service that will bring you all six new
Loveswept romances each month for the price of five—and
deliver them to you before they appear in the bookstores!

Examine 6 Loveswept Novels for

15 days FREE!

(SEE OTHER SIDE FOR DETAILS)

"It's no problem, Martha," Angelica said quickly. "I've grown very fond of him. In fact, I've even had fun. But please take your time and find him a really good home. Dan and I would be glad to have Patrick with us for as long as need be."

Dan strolled into the kitchen just in time to hear her last words. He immediately rushed over to her side.

"What?" he whispered, into her free ear. "What about Patrick staying?"

She motioned with her hand for him to be quiet, as Martha said, "We certainly appreciate all you've done for him, believe me. But we really are working very hard to find a suitable foster home."

"Martha, we don't want you to rush something through that might not be really good for the baby." Angelica gritted her teeth as Dan pulled the receiver away from her ear just enough for him to hear Martha's end of the conversation. "Patrick is certainly very content. He only fusses when he's hungry."

"Don't tell her that!" Dan whispered fiercely. "He's always hungry!"

"I beg your pardon?" Martha said.

Angelica glared at him, then turned away so she had a measure of privacy. "It was just Dan, adding his, ah . . . sentiments."

"I'll talk to you tomorrow," Martha said.

When Angelica hung up the phone, Dan fired off his questions.

"What's all this about Patrick?" he demanded. "Have they found a home for him?"

"No, not yet," she said, and glared at him. "Just

relax, Dan! Martha was only reassuring me that they were making an effort to find him a home."

"It sounded like they were getting close."

He looked as unhappy with the notion as she felt. She turned away and strolled over to the sliding glass doors. She had barely spoken to him all day because of his words on the beach, but this was something she shared with him. Maybe, she thought, knowing Dan wasn't as interested in her as she was in him would somehow make the reality about Patrick easier to face.

She was embarrassed now to realize that Dan didn't feel the same degree of attraction for her as she felt for him. She'd assumed . . .

Looking out on the fog-ladened evening, she forced her thoughts to more immediate matters and said, "I think they are getting something arranged soon. I . . . ah, expected it. After all, I can't really keep Patrick, no matter how much I like him."

"But you want to," Dan said softly, coming up behind her.

She swallowed back a lump of tears. "I—I don't know. I never thought it would hurt so much just to think of him leaving."

He put his hands on her shoulders and pulled her back against him. "Maybe we're both jumping to a conclusion here. You said they hadn't found anybody yet. Maybe it will be a while longer before they do."

His body was warm and comforting against hers, and she felt safe and protected . . . and cared for. It was an odd feeling, she thought, but it was what she needed at the moment. She allowed herself to open to it. She knew Dan was trying to calm and reassure her, and she liked that. The problem was that she couldn't afford to become too attached, as she had with Patrick.

Dan should be easier, she thought, slowly pulling away from him. He'd made it clear that he barely found her attractive. Now that ought to put a damper on any notions she might have had about her relationship with him.

"Angelica?"

"I'm okay." She turned around and forced herself to smile into the concerned brown gaze behind the tortoiseshell glasses.

"Are you sure?" he asked.

"Yes, I'm sure." Darn him, she thought. If he wasn't interested in her, then why did he look as if she were more than a business acquaintance or even a friend? "I'm just going to miss him, when he goes to his permanent home."

He nodded.

As she continued to gaze at him, she could feel a change in the air between them. Their mutual concern for a child was slowly being replaced by something else. She could sense a primitive desire rising, and found herself helplessly staring at his mouth. She had a desperate urge to show him that the passion in their kiss had been shared equally by both of them. He had to have felt that overwhelming, mind-spinning rush of emotions. She told herself she should be happy he had agreed with her that the kiss shouldn't be repeated, even if it wasn't for the same reason. She really ought to be pleased that this wouldn't be a conflict between them any longer.

She noticed he was silent, just looking down at her. His expression was unreadable.

She licked her lips unconsciously . . . and caught his eyes following the movement.

A rush of feminine power shot through her. Maybe he wasn't quite as detached as he claimed. Although her libido wanted to prove he was as attracted as she, she knew it would be wrong to do so. It really would. But maybe just a little personal satisfaction wouldn't be out of line.

She was about to reach out and touch his arm, when he smiled the politest, non-sexiest smile she'd ever seen.

"Well, since you're feeling better, I really should get back to my work," he said, patting her arm. "You were right about that, too. I expect to be in the den until very late. When you go up, would you leave the light next to the stairs on for me?"

"Sure," she muttered, wondering if she had imagined his interest.

"Great." To her annoyance, he strode out of the room whistling.

She was tempted to run after him and grab him and kiss him, just to see how mildly he reacted.

Dammit, she thought. She was more confused about him than ever. And if he kept this up much longer, she wouldn't be able to vouch for her sanity . . . or her self-control.

Seven

"Angelica, Clark says Mark IV has called again," Dan said, grinning at her as he held his hand over the receiver on the kitchen phone. "He thinks they sound frantic enough to get a good meeting out of them. What do you think?"

She lifted her head from feeding Patrick his morning bottle and gave him a heart-stopping smile. Dan felt his stomach tighten with desire.

"Well, we didn't plan it," she said, "but obviously this trip to the island has produced something unexpected. But I don't know if I can do a meeting. Not with Patrick."

Dan chuckled and winked at her. He took his hand away and said, "Clark, tell them we'll have to get back to them."

"But, Dan, we can't stall them forever!" Starlight's lawyer protested. "Mike Jimenez is asking for an answer today."

"Tell him we do want to reopen negotiations, but I can't give him an answer just yet. We'll call him next Monday to set up a date." He glanced at Angelica as he spoke.

"I suppose we can't put it off much longer," she said. "Not if we don't want to lose the deal altogether."

"If we have to, we'll bring Patrick to the meeting. Mark IV can meet the Chairman of the Board." Into the phone, he said, "Okay, Clark."

"I just wish you would tell me your game plan for this," Clark said. "I'd like to at least know what I'm supposed to be doing."

"When I know, Clark, you'll know."

"One of those, eh?"

Dan laughed at the man's conspiratorial tone. "One of those."

"One of those what?" Angelica asked as he hung up the phone.

"Seat-of-the-pants power plays," he said. He walked over to the counter and poured himself another cup of coffee.

"Oh, well, it's working beautifully so far," she said airily, then leaned forward and smiled. "Mark IV is very eager, Daniel."

Dan grinned at the gleam of anticipation in her eyes. The tigress was emerging. "I know. They shouldn't have showed that. So what do you think we can get this time?"

"I think," she pronounced with great satisfaction, "that they would change Patrick's diapers if we wanted it in the contract. But what about Garner? Will he be the negotiator again? If he is, I refuse to answer for my temper."

"Clark didn't say." Dan frowned. "He's been talking to Mike Jimenez, one of the vice presidents. I doubt, though, that they'll send Mitch again. The man blundered badly."

Her eyes narrowed. "The man was a preschool dropout, Dan."

"I believe you've mentioned that before." He smiled to himself as he remembered their first disastrous meeting with Garner.

She grinned crookedly at him. "I have the feeling you're not quite so angry with me about that mess anymore."

"No, not quite," he admitted, laughing.

As they continued to talk about the possible implications of Mark IV's continued interest in licensing Diana's game, Dan found his attention becoming more and more focused on her. He forced himself to ignore his body's reaction to her, just as he had for the past three days, ever since their late night mind-blowing kiss on the patio. It wasn't easy, though. The only thing that kept him sane was the hope that eventually it would all pay off.

So far, it seemed to be going well, he thought. He had noticed subtle changes in her. She was more open, and her eyes seemed to meet his more often. Also, she had acquired the disturbing habit of shifting her body . . . just as she was doing now. He watched her slowly uncross her legs and recross them. Her movements were just enough to draw his gaze, but not enough for him to judge if it was on purpose. She was doing something to her lips, too, he thought as his attention was captured by the faint moistness of her mouth. He didn't know what it was, but he loved it. He only hoped it wouldn't drive him insane.

Patrick finished his breakfast, bringing their business discussion to an end. However, talking was far from over, and Dan made a mental shift from sexy woman to innocent baby as "The Patrick Show" commenced. Both he and Angelica had started "talking" to the child after breakfast since Patrick was most awake then. The kid loved the attention, and Dan freely admitted he loved to watch the infant avidly follow every head and mouth movement.

". . . And Dan has to go and get you diapers," Angelica said sweetly to Patrick, who was staring at her wide-eyed.

"No, I don-n-n-n't," Dan singsonged, scowling at her.

"Yes, you do-o-o-o," Angelica singsonged back. "There's no room service here, Patrick, and that means good old Danny will discover the joys of running out for something every five minutes."

Angelica smiled brilliantly and Patrick laughed.

"But we brought a box of diapers with us—"

"And they're almost gone."

"What ever happened to liberated females, who can go to the store with the same equality as men?"

"They're running their practices and businesses and raising children at the same time. It's a feat beyond the scope of the male's ability, so that's why we send you guys out for diapers."

"Don't let her fill your head with that stuff, Patrick," Dan said to the baby.

"Are you going or aren't you?" Angelica asked, grinning at him.

"I'm going."

"See, Patrick? Dan had the opportunity to say no, and he blew it."

She rose from her seat, indicating "The Patrick Show" was over.

Dan patted her on the rear as she went by. "I'm a sucker for you, babe."

"What!" she gasped in shock, as much for his words as for his action.

"Since I'm relegated to the inferior male department, I figure I'm entitled to be a Neanderthal," he said. "And I think I'm going to like it."

Smiling in pleasure, he strolled out to get the diapers.

As Angelica settled into her paperwork a short time later, she admitted that getting a Neanderthal reaction from Dan did hold a certain satisfaction. At least he had *some* reaction to her.

It was enough that she knew it, she thought. That was all she wanted—just a little something that told her she was attractive to him. Okay, so now that she knew it, she could forget it. . . .

Instantly she felt again the sensation of his hand on her derriere.

"Forget it," she said out loud, and forced herself to focus on her work.

She wanted to get things in order before the "Today" show was over on the TV. Patrick was sitting in his rockerseat, watching as fixedly as any adult. Once the show was over, she knew he would cry that his friends had gone away. Besides, if she got her day's work organized she could take him for a morning outing without a guilty conscience.

She grinned as she thought of Dan on his way down to the village for some diapers. He wouldn't be too happy with her when he discovered she'd thought of the outing *after* he'd left on his errand.

She would promise to do the next two errands in apology . . . and combine them with outings for Patrick. Truthfully, neither she nor Dan had considered that option this morning.

To her amusement, when Dan returned with diapers, he was torn between annoyance with her for thinking of an outing, and annoyance with himself for not thinking of it. To her further amusement, he immediately opted to join her and Patrick for a stroll.

"We didn't have to go and buy another box of diapers," she said, as they were walking back up the road to the house hidden in the trees.

"Yes, we did," he said firmly. "I had to make the second trip count. Besides, I'll be damned before I'm running down to the general store every fifteen minutes for diapers."

She patted his arm. "Poor soul. You're lost without your room service."

"You loved it, too, and you know it."

She giggled.

As they came into sight of the house, they discovered a visitor waiting for them.

"It's about time," Martha said, as she rose from her makeshift seat on the redwood planter.

"What are you doing here?" they both asked in astonishment.

Martha was silent for an endless moment. Angelica felt her stomach plunge in fear.

"Can we go inside?" the woman finally asked. "I think we can talk better there."

Dan nodded. He walked around the stroller and opened the door. "Come in, Martha."

She nodded, then bent down and said to Patrick, "Hiya, hiya, Patrick. Have you been having fun here?"

Patrick smiled and happily kicked his feet. Angelica closed her eyes briefly at the endearing movement. Dammit, she thought. She had a pretty good idea why Martha had come, and she knew she was nowhere near ready for it.

Once inside the house, Angelica bitterly noticed that Martha smiled and chatted cheerfully about her ferry trip to Nadera. The woman was acting as if this were an everyday visit. And that meant something was seriously wrong.

In tense silence, she took a seat on the low-slung sofa, Patrick firmly held in her arms. Dan sat close to her, his thigh touching hers. He even put his arm around her, his fingers gripping her shoulder in comfort and concern.

"You're not here for a social call, Martha," Angelica said bluntly, when the woman was settled in a padded chair.

"No, I'm not," Martha said, breathing out a sigh. Her gaze was as measuring as the first time they had met, and Angelica fought the urge to panic.

"Have you come to take Patrick?" Dan asked.

It was out, Angelica thought dimly. He'd asked the question she was terrified to ask. His voice had been so deceptively calm that she couldn't help shuddering. She knew he was angry—extremely angry—and she realized that he was no more ready to let Patrick go than she was.

"No," Martha said.

"Thank goodness." Angelica sighed in immense relief. In the next instant, she glared at the woman. "Then why the hell are you here?"

"Because we have a problem about Patrick developing back in Seattle." Martha grimaced. "All the press about Patrick's discovery has resulted in several complaints about his placement with you two."

Angelica blinked in complete confusion. What was wrong with her and Dan that anybody could complain about?

"Martha, what are you talking about?" Dan asked, leaning forward. "What complaints?"

"Have you seen the newspapers yet today?"

They both shook their heads.

"Well, in two of them there are several letters to the editors that chastise the department for placing a baby in an 'immoral situation.' " Martha scowled fiercely. "One was quite explicit about, and I quote: 'the wanton corruption of an innocent baby by two people cohabiting in sin.' "

"Sin!" Angelica gasped, stiffening in outrage. "We are hardly cohabiting, let alone in sin!"

"Angelica!" Dan warned softly.

She ignored him as she continued their defense.

"You know as well as I do, Martha, that the law doesn't limit the placement of children to only married couples. Besides, Dan and I have never done anything! Anything! We hardly even—"

"We can hardly keep our hands off each other," Dan interrupted loudly, nudging her surreptitiously.

She gasped again, shocked by his words and confused by his actions. Then she realized that she had almost given away the truth of their "engagement." If there were trouble because they were "engaged," she could easily imagine the havoc it would cause if the truth were discovered.

"Okay, Martha," Dan went on, "so we're young and healthy and engaged to be married. Now why should that be a problem? Weren't those people ever young and healthy?"

"I doubt it," Martha said. "We've also had several phone calls complaining about Patrick being with you. Depending on the number who continue to lodge complaints, it might be cause for concern."

"Why would anyone even listen to such nuts?" Angelica asked in disgust.

"It all depends on how the nuts present their case," Martha said.

"So what do they want?" Dan asked.

"Basically, they all want Patrick to be moved to a home that's 'proper.' "

"That's ridiculous!" Angelica nearly shouted. "This is a proper home. These people don't give a damn about Patrick! They're just crazy publicity seekers who complain about everything and everyone."

"That's what the official feeling is right now."

"But will the department comply eventually?" Angelica asked angrily.

Martha was silent for a moment. "We don't want to."

"That's no answer," Angelica said, setting her jaw to hold back her fury.

"No, it isn't," Martha agreed. "I know I told you before that we were still working on finding a good home for Patrick. But this can raise quite a stink. I can't guarantee that the department won't bow to the pressure and move him before that."

"I'll begin a lawsuit," Angelica exclaimed. "We've been approved as Patrick's guardians. Dammit, you people investigated us thoroughly and gave us approval!"

"And you had custody of Patrick when we did it." Martha shrugged unhappily. "But remember, it was only temporary custody, so under the circumstances, the department may place him elsewhere."

"That's not fair!" Angelica felt tears press against her eyelids.

"It isn't right or fair for Patrick or us," Dan said. "If it's perfectly legal for us to have Patrick, then why the hell would the department even give credence to one or two individuals?"

"Normally, they wouldn't," Martha replied. "But a baby is an emotional issue, and we're afraid the question of improper placement might gain more public support. Also, we'll probably get volunteer families for Patrick—"

"But they won't care about him like we do," Angelica interrupted, twin tears spilling over. She refused to cry, she thought. Crying meant acceptance of the situation, and she would not accept this.

Dan's grip tightened on her shoulder, giving her strength. "What do we have to do to keep Patrick with us, Martha?" he asked.

"Yes," Angelica added, holding Patrick even more tightly. She inhaled the scent of innocent humanity; touched the soft infant skin; felt the small, warm body snuggled against her own. She wanted to scream out her anger and frustration at the unfairness being forced upon the child.

"Right now, nothing," Martha said. "There's really nothing that can be done. If it will make you two feel any better . . . I know I was cautious, but frankly I think Patrick's in a damn fine home now. And I think it would be a real sin to move him at all, pressure or no pressure."

"Thank you," Angelica said in a low voice.

"Take heart that the department isn't doing anything yet. As a matter of fact, we're not even asking you to return to Seattle unless you care to."

Angelica managed a smile. "Too bad we really can't skip over the border with him."

Martha shook her head, but she did smile back at her. "Tempting as that might be, don't even consider it. I really would put your heads on a pike. Look, I know this is unhappy news for you—it's tough not to get attached to the kids. That's why I came up here to talk to you personally, rather than over the phone."

"I'd like to say I appreciate that courtesy, Martha, but I can't," Dan said, his body stiff with emotion.

She nodded. "I understand. I wanted you to be prepared in case something did happen quicker than we all expected. And I wanted you to know how sorry I am about all this."

None of them had much to say after that. Even if they had, none felt like talking.

Angelica found herself moving like a robot for the next several hours, until Martha left for the return ferry to the mainland. She shouldn't have taken out her feelings on the social worker, she thought as she put Patrick down for his afternoon nap.

She leaned over the crib and watched the baby scoot a little on his belly to find a comfortable sleeping position. He was such a little thing to have so much controversy surround him, she mused. And worse, she had caused it. That she'd had a noble reason for doing it was no excuse. And this time the result was horrible.

There had to be something she could do to put things right. If she didn't, Patrick would be the one to pay for her mistake. At the moment, though, her emotions were on a roller coaster racing at one hundred miles per hour. She just couldn't get a grip on them to consider all the legal options that might be open—

Hundreds of families, she thought. Her brain told her at least one would be eminently qualified to care for Patrick. Her heart told her they wouldn't be nearly as good for him as she and Dan.

Patrick snuffled a whimper, and she realized her presence might be keeping him from sleep. She sighed and patted his thickly diapered rump, then walked out of the room.

Downstairs, she instantly headed for the patio.

She took a deep breath of sea-clean air in the hope that it would put her crumbling life back into perspective. It didn't. She could see a distant speck on the sea's horizon and wondered if it was the ferry.

A movement on the beach below caught her eye, and she gazed at the solitary figure walking slowly along the sand. She knew it was Dan, even though she hadn't seen him since he had taken Martha down to the ferry dock.

Lord, but she wished she had something other than her own arms around her in empty comfort. She knew how dangerous that wish was, but it still hurt to know that Dan hadn't come straight back to the house.

Eventually she saw him disappear into the trees and knew he was finally returning. She waited impatiently until he reappeared. He walked straight to her and wrapped her in a tight embrace.

For long silent minutes, he held her and she basked in his strength. She refused to admit that the embrace was anything more than the need for sympathy between human beings facing the same impending loss.

Finally, he let her go and turned to look out over the windswept straits. "We've got a problem."

"What Martha said?" she asked.

"Right. Even though they won't do anything for now, they will eventually. One way or another."

"I'm sorry," she said, her voice catching. She paused to regain her composure. "This is all my fault—"

"No, it's not," he broke in.

"I'm the one who started that stuff about being engaged."

"I've told you before that you didn't twist my arm."

"Dan, please." She rubbed her forehead to get rid of the sick ache. "We'll get into a fight if we keep disagreeing."

"As long as you stop taking the blame on yourself, I'll stop fighting," he said, and smiled slightly.

She drew in a deep breath and made a lame attempt at a joke. "Do you think we could sneak across the border with him?"

He actually chuckled. "And you a lawyer? Besides, I have a feeling Martha's on to it."

"Well, it seems like a logical solution to me."

"Unfortunately, it's one option we don't have."

"I was hoping not to hear that."

Dan turned and gazed at her. He could easily see the tears so close to the surface and the tremendous will she was exerting to hold them back. She had never looked more vulnerable than she did now. He had done a lot of thinking after he had dropped Martha off at the ferry. And he had come to a number of realizations. They had shocked him and he wasn't sure he was ready for all that they meant.

Finally he said, "One thing Martha's visit made me realize was that I can't let Patrick go. Even when you talked about bracing yourself for it, it still didn't really hit me that he might leave. I knew I was fond of him . . ."

"But you fell in love with him," she said, smiling sadly.

He set his jaw for a moment, trying to keep his control. "He feels right . . . he feels like he's mine. I didn't expect that."

"I know. I feel the same way." She bowed her head for a long minute, then straightened. "I can't believe they would even consider taking him away just because of a couple of letters and complaints from idiots."

The silence was thick between them. He stared at her profile. Her skin was like fine translucent marble, yet full of life. He knew so well the stubborn set to her jaw, the soft swell of her lips.

"What can we do?"

"There are some legal recourses concerning Patrick's welfare if he were moved . . . but the truth of our engagement would come out. The real problem would still be, though, that you and I . . . we're not a 'normal' family situation."

The silence was thicker and longer this time, and when it broke, it broke with all the fury of a hurricane.

"Marry me, Angelica."

Eight

The words were like a devastating punch to the solar plexus, and Angelica's mouth hung open in complete astonishment. "You can't be serious!"

"I am serious. Think about it, Angelica. People are complaining about us having Patrick because we're only engaged. But if we were married, who would complain then? Only real and true nuts, whom the press and the public could easily dismiss. Right now, it's being given credence because we aren't a normal family situation' for a baby."

Pain shot through her as she realized he was only asking her because of Patrick. What other reason would he have for asking her? she wondered. So why the hell should it hurt so much?

"Angelica."

She straightened, pushing away her bitter disappointment. "Yes?"

He blinked. "You mean you'll marry me?"

"No!" she exclaimed. Horrified at how much of her emotional state she gave away in that negative, she said very calmly, "I meant only a 'yes' to your saying my name. Dan, it's insane to get married just for the sake of a baby."

"Then you tell me another way we can stop the complaints as effectively," he demanded.

"We can . . . well, if we . . . maybe . . ." She wracked her brain, but she couldn't think straight. No wonder, she thought in frustration. Dan had thrown her one hell of a surprise.

He crossed his arms over his chest. "Can't think of anything, can you?"

"Dammit, Dan," she said, swiping the air with one hand. "Marriage is a very serious step."

"Patrick is a very serious business."

"But there's no guarantee that we could keep Patrick, even if we did get married."

"Sure, we could. I'll bet that's exactly what Martha was after. I think she was hinting at it when she said she thought Patrick was doing just fine where he was. And she kept emphasizing that us not being married was the root of the protest. She'll be back in Seattle in a couple of hours. We can call her and check."

"But there could still be protests."

"You said yourself the law was on our side. If we make sure the media gets invited to the wedding, they'll play it up. Any further complaints wouldn't have a legitimate leg to stand on."

The word "marriage" kept sweeping through her

mind, keeping her from thinking properly. Dan was so good with Patrick, she thought. And he could provide everything a child could need and want. So could she. Whether she was good with Patrick . . . well, she tried damn hard. She could at least teach him to strive for a goal. She had to admit they even seemed to have Martha's blessing.

"It's not right," she said, trying to hang on to some semblance of common sense. "Dan, we wouldn't be marrying for the right reasons."

"Patrick needs this, Angelica," he said, resting his hands on her shoulders. "Look at the way he's thrived and been happy in our care. We've been good for him, and we would *know* he'd continue to get that kind of care because it would be us doing it. If there were anybody who wanted Patrick, like his mother or father or other relatives, they would have claimed him by now. If they haven't after all the press so far, they're not going to. We can't allow him to be taken away because someone complains that we're an unorthodox arrangement."

"You're letting your emotions run away with you, Dan." She was so tempted by what he was saying that she had to stop him.

"Why shouldn't I? I'm entitled to be a little emotional. I've made a lot of sacrifices for him already, and done it gladly."

She couldn't help a dry chuckle. "You sound like you just finished paying for a full four years at Harvard."

"Why not?" he said, grinning at her. "No reason in the world why he can't go to Harvard or MIT or

CalPoly or the University of Vienna, even." His grin faded. "I can't face giving him up. Can you?"

She fought to hold herself in control. It was as if the world had suddenly turned upside down.

"No," she said. "But marriage—"

"Look, I know it's a surprise. Why don't you think about it?"

"You're the one who should think about it," she muttered.

"Dammit, Angelica, just give it a chance!" he snapped. "We'd probably be better at marriage than most people because we'd know exactly what we're getting into."

With that, he turned around and strode into the house.

Angelica found her hands trembling and immediately tucked them under her top. In spite of the warm sun, she felt cold as ice.

Just the thought of marriage was frightening to her. She could so easily recall two embittered adults fighting in a courtroom over children. Dan wasn't in his right mind, she thought frantically. He couldn't be to have suggested such a drastic step. That was it, she decided. He was crazy . . . and, Lord, but she wanted to be crazy with him.

She thought of a client, a couple actually, who had married for business purposes. She knew they were fond of each other and they seemed content with their lives. But more important, they were still married after eight years. As their business lawyer, Angelica would be the first to know about an imminent divorce.

Maybe it was the marrying for love that was the problem, she thought. Maybe when the love died, there was nothing to hold two people together. Maybe if only she weren't so attracted to Dan, she wouldn't be confused about everything else. If only she could be sure that what she felt for him was merely a strong fondness. . . .

"What are you doing, you idiot!" she exclaimed aloud, pressing her hands to her temples in an effort to clear her head of its ridiculous thought.

She was becoming as crazy as Dan, and it had to stop. Marriage to keep Patrick was tempting, but there were no guarantees it would work. The 'what ifs' ran through her head like wildfire. It was too risky for more reasons than she cared to think about.

Five minutes later, she was standing in front of Dan as he sat at his desk in the den.

"What about our businesses?" she asked.

He adjusted his glasses. "Well, I think it would depend on whose business was most easily movable. It's only common sense."

"Let's face it, mine is the easiest."

"Does this mean you've thought about it?"

"I think the whole idea is insane."

She walked out of the den.

A short time later, she was back.

"Would you consider a prenuptial agreement?"

"Of course," he said, looking up from his computer.

She walked out again.

"It's all wrong," she said, back in the den once more.

Dan drew in a deep breath and leaned back in the chair. "Is it wrong that we love Patrick, and we both want the very best for him? And if we can do that by being married, then why not? Let's face it, the oldest reason in the world to get married is to have children. People have been doing it for thousands of years."

"Oh."

She walked out again . . . and turned right around and walked back in.

"What about—?"

"Dammit, Angelica!" Dan roared, slapping the desk with his open palms. "Just say yes!"

"Yes."

She blinked in astonishment.

"Thank you," Dan said, much more quietly, while sinking back into his swivel chair. "I'm happy to marry you, too."

She swallowed. "But—"

"No buts," he said sternly. "You accepted, and I am holding you to it."

She closed her eyes for a long minute as confusion overwhelmed her. She was so afraid, for herself, for Dan, and for Patrick. And her pride was battered at his asking her to marry him for the sake of a baby.

She told herself that Patrick was her main motive for accepting. Marriage was the quickest solution to the current situation . . . provided certain provisions were worked out.

"I think it would be for the best if we thought of this as a 'child' arrangement," she said, gathering her control about her.

His eyes narrowed. "What do you mean?"

"We're marrying for Patrick's sake, right?"

He nodded cautiously.

"I think we should agree to stay married at least until we're all sure there won't be any more complaints, then we can . . . reevaluate the situation."

"What the hell are you talking about?" Dan asked, rising from his chair.

"I'm talking about a little caution!" she exclaimed, backing away as he began to pace the room. "I'm only suggesting that we use some common sense here. For goodness' sake, what if we discover the marriage won't work? We ought to acknowledge that quickly, and we should make some kind of provision for that in the prenuptial agreement."

Dan cursed under his breath. Leave it to Angelica to turn a marriage proposal into a business negotiation, he thought angrily. Why couldn't she just accept that she had said yes? Thousands of women did it every day.

Thousands of women weren't Angelica.

So much for not rushing her, he thought wryly. But, unfortunately, events hadn't waited for wooing, and he had been forced to act quickly or lose the two most important people in his life.

The calmer part of his mind reminded him that she hadn't taken back her answer. She wanted the marriage. That she was being cautious was only to be expected.

He wished he had expected it, but he hadn't thought beyond getting a "yes" from her. Now all he had to do was get her married. At the moment, that was his prime objective . . . for more than one reason.

"Fine," he said, even though the word left a bad taste in his mouth.

She stared off into space, and in that instant, satisfaction roared through him. He waited, however, for her to tell him what he'd already guessed.

"Then I think I can marry you," she finally said.

"Good."

Dan resisted the urge to smile.

"Next Saturday."

Angelica swallowed hard as she heard Dan inform the hotel manager of the wedding date. They had stopped at the front desk for the suite keys and the manager had inquired about their trip to the island.

It was official now, she thought. She automatically tightened her grip on Patrick.

"Can the hotel help you in any way with your wedding plans?" the manager asked eagerly. "We can arrange any kind of wedding reception that would suit you."

Dan turned and gave her a lopsided grin. "Our families will probably want to come."

"Sure," she muttered. "They were so thrilled about the engagement, they wouldn't dare miss the wedding."

He gave her a warning look.

She cleared her throat and said to the manager, "We haven't really thought of planning anything. . . ."

"But it's your wedding!" the manager exclaimed. "Surely, you'd like a special dinner at least?"

"Oh . . . ah . . . well." She looked helplessly at Dan.

"We'll let you know exactly what we want tomorrow," Dan said, and ushered her toward the elevators.

"Dammit," she said in disgust, when they were finally alone in the suite. "Why didn't we think to call the families?"

"We're just getting used to the notion ourselves." He patted her back. "You're doing fine, Angelica."

"I wish I had your confidence."

"Hey, Martha and her boss have confidence in us, so why shouldn't I?"

It was quite true that Martha, when they had informed her the day before of the impending nuptials, had issued hearty congratulations. She'd also confided that she'd hoped for it. Martha was making it very clear that she thought Patrick's temporary guardians should be his permanent ones.

Patrick, Angelica thought dryly, had done it again. She kissed his forehead and admitted he was worth it. He'd better be, because she and Dan were committed now. She began to strip off his clothes to get him ready for bed.

"We better call our parents tonight," she said, then groaned. "Your mother will be jumping for joy."

Dan laughed. "Leave my mother to me."

She started to laugh too. "We spent all that time on the island working out all the details of the marriage, and we forgot about telling anybody."

"Probably we both figured telling Martha was enough," he said, as he began putting away all their paraphernalia. "We'll have a small dinner after the ceremony. Just our families, maybe a few of my executives—"

"No!" she exclaimed, turning around while keeping one hand on the baby. "Dan, this isn't a normal marriage."

"Angelica, everyone will expect it, and it would certainly put an end to any speculation about us. Besides, how many times does a person—barring Elizabeth Taylor—get married?"

She turned back around without answering. She couldn't do a wedding reception, she thought furiously. She had a business to move up here and she had to get ready for new negotiations with Mark IV. Possibly, even some house hunting, too. The marriage would be more than enough. No way, nohow, nowhere would she deal with a wedding, too.

Angelica pushed Patrick's stroller through the heavy doors of the bridal boutique.

"Okay," she muttered. "So I'm not Elizabeth Taylor."

"Hellew," drawled an elegantly dressed older woman. "How may I help you?"

"I need a dress for a wedding," Angelica said, watching Patrick drop his teething ring onto the rug. Absently, she bent down and picked it up, wiped it off, and handed it back to him.

"Ah, something for the matron of honor," the woman said. "Gown or street-length?"

Angelica frowned. What matron of . . .

"No," she said quickly. "I'm the one getting married."

"Congratulations!" the woman exclaimed, smiling broadly. "Now I have some lovely street-length dresses that are very appropriate for second marriages."

"This is a first marriage."

The woman blinked, glanced at Patrick, and smiled politely. "I see. Well, let me show you what I have."

Angelica began to follow her to the back of the shop, when she felt the stroller suddenly swing toward the right. Glancing down, she discovered to her horror that Patrick had grabbed a handful of delicate French lace on the skirt of an obviously expensive tea-length wedding gown. He had it in his mouth, and was sucking on the material.

"Oh, no, Patrick!" Angelica cried in dismay.

"Omigod!" the woman exclaimed, turning back to see what was keeping her customer. "That's a Priscilla Original."

Angelica cursed under her breath as she knelt down and attempted to disentangle the baby from the gown.

"It's ruined! It's ruined!" the woman screeched, dancing around the stroller in her agitation.

Angelica sighed and uttered the words that soothed salespeople everywhere. "I'll pay for it."

It couldn't get any worse, she staunchly told herself as she glared at a happily grinning Patrick.

Three hours later, Angelica pushed the stroller into Starlight Software's downtown offices. Everyone turned and stared as she strode with single-minded determination toward the executive offices. When she reached the one marked President, she gritted her teeth in towering anger and satisfaction and shoved open the door.

"Can I help you, Ms. Windsor?" Dan's secretary asked, looking up from her keyboard.

"Not likely," she muttered, forcefully wheeling the stroller toward the inner office door.

"He's having a meeting!" the secretary called out, rising from her desk.

Ignoring the woman, Angelica pushed the door open and the stroller through. She had a vague impression of a couch and chairs lined with people, then all her attention was focused on the man behind the large desk.

"Angelica!" Dan exclaimed, standing abruptly.

"You take him!" she said, maneuvering the stroller around the desk. "You want a wedding with all the trimmings, then you can look after this—this miniature Dennis the Menace so that the bride can at least get a dress!"

"Calm down, Angelica," Dan began.

"I will not calm down! How am I supposed to manage this when he eats two-thousand-dollar originals, screams at the top of his lungs because he's hungry, and then refuses to take his bottle?"

"I'm sorry you're having a bad time with him," Dan said, glaring at her. "But—"

"Don't," she said in the sweetest of voices. "Just don't."

She glanced down at her tormentor, who in turn

smiled angelically at her. She growled, whipped around, and marched out of the office, muttering, "I ought to divorce the both of them before the wedding begins."

"Angelica! Angelica!"

"Forget it, Dan. You've got him for the rest of the day!"

Having given her final statement, she smiled grimly and walked out the door.

The wedding was perfect. The groom was handsome and quietly determined. The bride was beautiful and unexpectedly shy. The mothers cried on cue. And the best man sucked loudly on his bottle throughout the entire ceremony.

Well, it was almost perfect, Dan thought, grinning as he pulled up Patrick's pants after changing the baby's diaper in his bedroom.

Adam Roberts looked over his younger brother's shoulder and said, "That didn't look so bad."

"I could tell you tales, big brother," Dan said, laughing at Adam's reaction to a barely dirty diaper. "And I'm not about to."

Adam chuckled. "I don't think I want to know. I have a feeling Diana and I would be too scared to have kids if we did know. I've got to admit he's a real charmer."

Dan smiled at Patrick. "Uncle Adam should have been around the other day, when you almost lost me a bride."

"What?"

"Never mind."

There was no sense explaining Angelica's prewedding explosion, Dan thought. His brother probably wouldn't understand it. Adam's wife, Diana, had a much more calm nature than Angelica. Very calm, in fact. She and Angelica were such opposites, it was hard to believe they were cousins.

Still, he was relieved the wedding had come off at all—especially after the onset of Angelica's bridal nerves. It had been a horrible shock when she'd stormed into his office with Patrick and stormed back out again without him. He'd arrived home from the office and nearly panicked to find the suite empty. Then he'd realized all her things were still there, so he waited as patiently as possible for her to return. She had, subdued and slightly embarrassed . . . and without a dress for the wedding. She had avoided looking him in the eye and said, "Patrick's dress was the best." They both burst into laughter.

She hadn't apologized for her blowup in his office, and he admitted she hadn't needed to. After all, she'd been under a tremendous strain, and was entitled to it. That there had been only one was a miracle really. He had considered it a wise move not to tell her belatedly that the hotel offered baby-sitter services. She probably wouldn't have appreciated it then.

"Are you sure about all this?" Adam asked, breaking into his thoughts.

"Yes."

He felt as if he had fought a major battle to earn

the right to say that firmly and without hesitation. He wasn't a reluctant groom. Things had happened so fast that maybe he hadn't had time to have second thoughts, but he doubted that. Lately, he'd had a growing sense of rightness that had culminated in the legal commitment today.

Adam stared at him for a long moment. "Okay. It's just that this is an . . . unusual marriage. By the way, Dad thinks Angelica has great legs."

Dan grinned. "I know."

Adam grinned back. "Diana and I support you two. We think you're crazy, but we're with you. In fact, Diana is out in the sitting room right now being crazy on your behalf—"

"Dan?"

He turned at the sound of Angelica's voice. She stood in the doorway of his bedroom. Her satin wedding gown was the palest of cream and almost the epitome of modesty with its long sleeves and full skirt gathered into a dropped waist. Almost, Dan thought, as he found his gaze focusing helplessly on the deep cleavage revealed by the sheer lace that comprised the upper portion of the bodice. The dress was also subtly sexy in the way it enhanced the curves of her body, molding to her breasts and waist before flaring out over her hips.

Her left hand was touching the doorjamb, and her square-cut emerald engagement ring and gold wedding band glinted richly in the late afternoon light.

He was a lot of things, Dan admitted, but crazy wasn't one of them. As he gazed at the ring, he suppressed yet again the thought that a wedding was always followed by a wedding night. Whether this one would or not was a question that had burned in him since she'd agreed to marry him.

"Are you done with Patrick?" she asked. "Martha wants more pictures before she leaves."

"I suppose we owe her," he said, holding the baby out to his new wife.

"You like her, Danny, and you know it," she said sternly.

He saw his brother's eyebrows shoot up at the nickname and hid a smile.

The smile immediately subsided when he noticed a tightness around Angelica's mouth that hadn't been there before. "Is something wrong?"

Her gaze slid to Adam, then back to him. "No. I'm just tired, I suppose."

After Angelica and Patrick left the room, Adam said, "Interesting."

"What?" Dan asked, gazing after his new family.

"Seeing Angelica with a baby. By the way, I've heard that babies refuse to allow adults a sex life."

Dan stared at his brother in horror. It couldn't be true, he thought wildly.

Adam shrugged. "It's probably one of those 'wive's tales'."

Dan gulped in air. "I expect so."

"You better hope so," Adam said, laughing. "You look like a starving man with the feast in sight."

He was, Dan acknowledged. Under other circumstances, his starvation should come to an end tonight. He forced the thought away.

As they left the room, Dan made a mental note to

question Angelica further and find out what was bothering her, but he didn't have the chance until after everyone had left and they had put Patrick to bed.

"I will never do that again," Angelica said. Her voice was low with fury as she walked into her kitchenette, the skirt of her wedding gown swirling about her ankles.

"What?" Dan asked in astonishment, following after her. "What's wrong?"

"Having a wedding dinner for twenty people and the families back here afterward," she answered angrily as she started fixing the morning coffee. She literally threw the ingredients together, and he was vaguely surprised that her gown came through it undamaged. The counter was covered with spilled coffee grounds and water. She turned around and leaned on the counter.

"Did something happen?" he asked suspiciously. "Did anyone say anything to you? My mother?"

"Nothing happened," she snapped. "Unless you count my feeling like a hypocrite. People were congratulating me and wishing me the best. Even my own mother said how wonderful the ceremony was. For goodness' sake, she knows we got married only for Patrick!"

Dan knew her mother had probably been putting on her best for the occasion. They had been forced to confess the true situation to their immediate families. That none of them was too pleased was an understatement. Not that he cared a damn what the families thought. "Angelica, did you ever think that maybe it was a nice ceremony?"

"We shouldn't have had anyone to the wedding," she said. "The two of us before the judge would have been just fine."

"We only had the people closest to us here."

"And Martha!" she exclaimed, slicing the air with her hand. "Who brought the press."

"You knew she was doing that." He could feel his own temper rise. "You, if I remember correctly, were positively beaming as you answered their questions during that short interview!"

She ignored him. "All that other stuff was unnecessary. The champagne at dinner, the little wedding cakes, the hors d'oeuvres and wine here at the suite. It was too much fuss under the circumstances."

He sensed that she was deliberately provoking a fight, and he had no idea why. This was not the kind of wedding night he'd envisioned. It certainly wasn't the one he'd hoped for.

"Angelica," he said, his voice low in warning, "the damn hotel did that, and you know it. I think you had better end this 'discussion' right now."

To his irritation, she ignored him again. "If it had been a normal wedding and we had chosen not to have any guests, nobody would have thought twice about it. But we're not a normal couple who got married for all the normal reasons, and we shouldn't have acted like we were."

"I don't understand you," he said, his temper beginning to fray. "We did what was expected—"

"And that's what I'm upset about," she broke in.

"Because now we're going to be expected to do a lot more normal married things. But it isn't ever going to be normal."

The word "normal" screeched across his nerves and gouged into him. It defied him like the bullfighter's red cape defying the bull.

"You want normal," he said, reaching out blindly and grasping her upper arms. "I promise you, Angelica Roberts, you will have a normal marriage. Now."

Nine

Angelica stiffened in momentary astonishment as Dan's mouth came down on hers in a devastating kiss. She knew she should protest, but she couldn't seem to move her muscles. The little voice that was usually so insistent on the side of caution and common sense was barely audible and fading fast. Part of her was shocked that he would kiss her like this. Part of her leaped with joy that he did.

His lips moved across her fiercely, and he pulled her tightly against his hard body. Her mouth adjusted itself to his in automatic response, and she sagged against him. Her body was already pushing against his in instinctive feminine reaction. She could feel every inch of him—the iron wall of his chest, the pressure of his belly, the long line of his thighs. The tautly strung tension of weeks of awareness was releasing and rewinding into a tight coil of sensuality.

The ache that began in her breasts spread through her ribs, past her belly and settled in her thighs. Her arms crept around his shoulders, her fingers digging into his skin. She parted her lips to the kiss, and their tongues swirled together, igniting the fire of emotions inside her. His arms were steel bands about her back, enclosing her in a lure of promise and heartbreak.

When he raised his head a long time later, she slowly opened her eyes. He was gazing down at her in male triumph. She knew he was pleased with her revealing response to him, and his words about his easily being able to control his attraction came rushing back. So did the hurt.

"You want this," he said in a low, raspy voice.

"Damn you, Daniel Roberts," she whispered, furious with him for proving his point so easily. "You turn me inside out."

"And you make me crazy."

Anger and desire warred within her for an instant longer, and the desire won out. She plowed her fingers through his hair and pulled his mouth back down to hers. This morning she had truly realized that she would be facing a wedding night. The thought had frightened her, and she had tried to provoke a fight with him to prevent it.

Instead, she'd provoked this, and she was glad. She wanted him. She didn't even care that she shouldn't. She remembered the way they had laughed together over the wedding dress fiasco, and knew she had grown closer to him since then. The emerald ring was heavy on her third finger, making her aware of a number of things at once. She had entered into one kind of union with Daniel Roberts today. Maybe she was entitled to another, much more primitive kind. But he had to want her just as much, she thought dimly. Not just as a marriage partner for Patrick's sake, but her for herself. She was entitled to that, too.

She let the last of her control go and instinct took over. Her body flowed into his, her hands seeking out the hidden strength of his shoulders. Her mouth teased and turned, then offered as much as it took.

Dan shuddered violently. She found an intense satisfaction at his impatient touch. And then she was lost when his fingers curved around her breast. They explored and measured, paid special attention to the puckering nipple.

She moaned as a savage need shot through her. She had never expected to feel this kind of passion for any man. It frightened her at the same time it left her breathless for more.

She moaned again as Dan strung kisses down her neck and across the valley of her breasts. His mouth grazed hotly across her skin, covered only by lace. He teased at the curving plumpness of her breasts, revealed by the deep V of her bodice. Her hands guided him, and the intensity of the pressure building inside her was shocking. It throbbed hotly throughout her in a wave of unstoppable force. She was spinning into mindless confusion. The sensations were close to insanity, and yet she didn't want them to end.

Dan let out an unsteady breath. He couldn't believe the incredible softness of her flesh, the sweet taste that was Angelica. All thoughts of a slow wooing were forgotten. He could only remember that she was his. He had a claim to her now that no other man could have. She needed to know that, he thought dimly. But even as his hands traveled slowly over her buttocks, he was aware that a kitchenette was not the place to make love.

Reluctantly he raised his head and straightened. A hard fist seemed to slam into his body when he saw the delicate flush on her beautiful face, the languid heat in her eyes, the soft bruising of her lips from the kiss. He wanted her so badly that the thought of the few yards to one of the bedrooms was almost dampening. He didn't think he could wait that long.

He lifted her in his arms. Her eyes widened at the sudden movement.

"Dan!" she gasped, clutching at his neck for balance. "What are you doing?"

"Being romantic," he said, grinning at her. "Now, be quiet. We have to sneak past Patrick."

She blinked in confusion, then grinned back at him, her eyes brimming with sensual amusement. He quickly crept through the sitting room toward his bedroom. He held his breath as he tiptoed past the crib. Patrick didn't move, clearly sound asleep. Patrick had to cooperate tonight, Dan thought. He wondered if children always created this kind of havoc with their parents, then decided it was only because he had started their lovemaking in the wrong spot. He really wished he hadn't. Now Angelica would have time for second thoughts. He didn't want second thoughts. Not tonight.

After entering the bedroom, he nudged the door shut with one foot. He leaned against it and stared into Angelica's eyes. He couldn't see her expression in the darkness. He released her legs, while keeping one arm tight about her waist. Her body slid slowly down his, the movement arousing him in ways he hadn't conceived of.

"Let's start a good marriage," he whispered. "You and I."

"Marriage can hurt," she whispered back.

"I won't hurt you," he vowed.

She didn't answer. It was an acquiescence, and he wasn't foolish enough to ask for more. Instead, he took her mouth in a kiss designed to restoke the fires. It did, with magnificent results.

Her mouth fused to his. Her hands tortured him as they pushed his jacket off, then slipped beneath his shirt. The buttons seemed to dissolve under her touch, and then her fingers were trailing heat through the hair on his chest. He couldn't control his own hands as they kneaded her breasts with a shocking lack of finesse. Rather than pull away, she met him with honest need.

He walked her backward to the bed, urged her down onto it, and sprawled atop her. He gasped as her breasts pressed into his chest, the nipples diamond-hard points that teased him into a throbbing frenzy. He buried his mouth against them, tasting every inch of skin. He stripped her clothes from her as he explored her body with frantic hands. Her thighs flowered open under his touch, leaving him dizzy with her willing response.

And she gave. Her hands weren't content just to hold him. They caressed his back and chest with a tender frenzy that matched his own. They trailed lower, her nails raking his flesh lightly, bringing him to the brink of insanity. Her body was silken heat against his, and he gloried in it. He had known it would be like this . . . and yet he was stunned by its depths. The thought was lost as her thighs rubbed with increasing supplication against his. The last shreds of his control broke, and he sank into her. She enfolded him with feminine grace, moving with him in an undeniable point and counterpoint of commitment. The rightness of it pounded through him, forcing its way into every small particle of him. His heart acknowledged what his body had always known. The want and the need wrapped together, and he knew that even in a lifetime he would never get enough of her.

Emotion swirled through Angelica, capturing her in its maelstrom. She was helpless to resist it. She met every thrust with an equal one of her own. Each time she felt the power of their lovemaking course through her, pulling more and more of her heart with it. She wanted to cry out her denial . . . and instead cried out her pleasure as a brilliant light burst through her over and over again. Then Dan was joining her in the fury, holding her, keeping her anchored and yet free.

And then came ecstasy . . . and its aftermath of sweet, soothing peace.

Long minute later, Angelica slowly opened her eyes. She felt weightless and floating. Nothing seemed to matter, and she basked in that.

Slowly she became aware of the cool breeze of conditioned air . . . and the hard male body atop hers. Her husband.

The breath squeezed out of her in a rush, and she gasped at the sudden vise in her chest.

Dan shifted his weight and kissed her cheek. "Angelica? I . . . Did I hurt you?"

She shook her head, although her mind was flashing images at her of courtrooms and families torn apart. Their lovemaking had been too intense. She'd given too much of herself up to it. . . .

"No, you're not okay," he said, placing both his hands on her temples and making her face him. "I'm sorry. I shouldn't have . . . forced this issue."

"You didn't force anything," she said, halting his apology. She had to correct him on that. "I—I wanted this tonight. I would be lying if I said differently."

"And now you're going to tell me it won't happen again," he said, his tone very dry.

She stilled instantly. The intimacy of their positions made her all too aware of what he meant. She also became aware of her nudity . . . and his. He couldn't see her, she thought, while feeling a hot blush spread across her face and chest. But he could certainly feel her. All over. Just as she could feel him.

Immediately, she wanted to make love again. It was like opening a floodgate of repression. And she had repressed a lot of physical attraction for this man. It was only now, after tasting the incredible intimacy, that she knew how much.

"No," she said. "I'm not going to say that."

"I've been thinking that maybe we should give this marriage a chance, Angelica," he said, brushing the hair back from her face. "I think you know as well as I do that there's more between us than Patrick."

"Is there?" she asked. "We fight about everything, Danny. We don't even agree on what kind of juice we should have at the breakfast table."

"That's why we always have both." He nuzzled her throat. "Keep calling me Danny, and I will buy you a juice factory. I love the way you say my name."

She swallowed, realizing how much she'd taken to calling him that lately. It was funny how one recognized an unconscious habit once it was pointed out.

"I know you feel . . . rushed," he said.

"I feel scared," she admitted bluntly. "I've had complete control over my life since college, and then I came here and lost it. Completely and totally lost it. Worse, I've had a hand in the process!"

He chuckled.

"It isn't funny, Dan." She pushed at his shoulders. "Will you let me up?"

He trailed kisses across her cheek and under her ear. She gasped and arched her back in instinctive reflex as a bolt of lightning hurtled through her. He concentrated on a particularly erogenous spot until she was writhing beneath him.

"I think that with half a chance we'll make a marriage, Angelica," he said, lifting his head. "I won't let you up until you agree to give it that chance. We've learned a lot about each other lately, including how to compromise. Besides, if we're going to evaluate the situation eventually, we've got to have all the facts, don't we?"

She felt her cheeks flush hotly. "I'll try," she finally said.

"And I know I'll try my absolute best. Just like this."

His lips again found the sensitive spot behind her ear. She arched immediately.

"Mmmm," he murmured, nibbling on her earlobe. "If the wedding night is any indication, then we're well on our way to a normal marriage."

"Dan," she said breathlessly, her hands gripping his shoulders tightly as desire, thick and hot, swirled through her. "I have the feeling . . . this will hardly be a normal marriage."

"I think you're right."

"Hi, Angelica. What's for dinner?"

Angelica shook her head at Dan's greeting as he came into the suite.

"What we have every night for dinner," she said. "Room service."

"Now, would 'Father Knows Best' have room service?" he asked dryly.

"No," she admitted cheerfully. "But you would. Shall I get the menu?"

"Surprise me tonight." He walked over to Patrick in his rockerseat and ruffled the child's silky-fine hair. "Hiya, kid. You been a good boy today?"

"Lord," Angelica muttered. Dan was pushing a TV show image of family life a little too much. "He'll be wanting to get a dog next."

"What?" Dan asked, straightening.

"Oh, ah . . ." Dammit, she thought as her brain scrambled for an answer of sorts. "I was wondering aloud if I wanted a hot dog for dinner."

He set his briefcase down on the coffee table. "A hot dog?"

"Yes. I don't know." She shrugged.

He came over to her and took her in his arms. "I missed you."

She smiled up at him. He was so determined to make a normal marriage out of this bizarre situation. Remembering the past seven glorious nights, she admitted she was enthusiastically giving this relationship a chance herself. Still, there was a part of her heart that held back. . . .

She instantly forgot her musings when his lips found hers in a much more intimate greeting. She was breathless when he finally lifted his head.

"You certainly know how to say 'hello,' " he whispered.

"So do you."

A high-pitched squeal drew their reluctant attention. Patrick had dropped his teething ring again. Knowing the moment was gone, Angelica broke away from Dan and tended the baby.

"So how's the outside world?" she asked as she straightened.

"Hectic." He loosened his tie and flopped down on the sofa. "Boy, am I bushed."

"Shall I make you a drink?" she asked, figuring that was what a normal wife would ask. She had promised to make this work, and she would.

He glanced at her. "Thanks. I really appreciate that. A beer would be great."

The surprise in his voice left her feeling vaguely ashamed. She knew she'd made the offer unenthusiastically. She got a beer from the small refrigerator in the kitchenette and handed it to him. As she turned to leave he reached out and pulled her down next to him.

"Dan!" she protested.

He grinned. "I'll be nice and make dinner."

She had to laugh. "That's a major sacrifice in this household."

"I know. You could get warped fingers from dialing the phone." He bent over and unstrapped Patrick from his rockerseat. Setting the baby on the sofa with him, he added, "How are you doing with moving your practice?"

She groaned. "I'm still sorting through my California clients. I have more than I thought. Only about twenty percent are here in Washington."

"You could always take on a California partner, or sell that end of the practice, couldn't you?"

Instantly, she felt her temper rise at the suggestion. She suppressed it. A normal marriage meant remaining calm at all times. "I really don't want to do that, Dan. Anyway, my practice is mostly paperwork. I think I can work it out eventually."

"Remember, I'll be glad to help you."

She smiled sweetly. "Of course."

"Speaking of your clients, Mark IV called again. I set up a meeting for early next week."

"You—" She instantly clamped her mouth shut over her protest. After all, she had known that another meeting was inevitable. But it would have been nice if Dan had consulted with her before setting a date. This was exactly the kind of thing that had made him seem as if he were against her before. She felt remnants of her old wariness return, and immediately forced them away. Much as she wanted to yell at him, she only asked, "What day next week?"

"I left that open until I could talk to you."

"I see."

"I had to give them something, Angelica," he snapped. "They have been very patient with us."

"I just said 'I see,' " she said, holding onto her fraying temper. "I'm concerned about handling a meeting."

"I'm sorry," he said, kissing her cheek in apology. "Do you want me to call them back and cancel?"

She smiled and shook her head. "No. I'm just nervous about it."

He kissed her again. "You'll be fine. Knowing you, you'll be terrific."

His mouth trailed lower to her neck, and suddenly she was fighting for air. "Dan, the baby."

He straightened reluctantly. "The sacrifices I make."

"Well, make another one," she said, grinning at him. "Call room service. I'm starving."

It wasn't quite a normal marriage, Dan admitted as he watched Angelica smile sweetly at the new representative from Mark IV Computers. But it wasn't dull.

"I'm sure, Mr. Jimenez, that we can come to satisfactory terms," she said, shifting Patrick onto her shoulder and gently burping him. "For the right price."

Mike Jimenez's eyebrows rose. "Ms. Windsor, I was hoping that we had reached those satisfactory terms with the last negotiations."

"Mrs. . . . Roberts," she corrected him gently, and glanced over at her husband. "But please call me Angelica."

Dan grinned back and decided just to let her go. Poor Jimenez didn't know what to do with her anyway. Actually, the man didn't know what to do with the entire meeting, since he was the only one disconcerted by the presence of a baby.

Patrick gave the obligatory burp, and Angelica said, "What a good bunny, Patrick. Now, Mike . . . May I call you Mike?"

The man nodded, almost in awe at the way she was switching roles. No one would have guessed that she'd been nervous about this meeting, Dan thought as he rose to take Patrick from her.

"You're doing great," he whispered in her ear,

then turned to Jimenez. "Excuse me, Mike. I have to put the Chairman of the Board down for his afternoon nap."

Jimenez smiled and nodded, although his attention was on Angelica.

Smart man, Dan thought, as he carried Patrick into the nursery. She was charming him, and he knew it.

"Think she'll get a hell of a deal, Patrick?" he asked. He bobbed the baby's head up and down. "Yes, my lad. I thought so too. Be sure and wangle a new teddy bear out of her after she gets her commission from Diana."

He put the baby in the crib on his tummy and gently patted the diapered backside. Mark IV had been very insistent on a meeting this week. They were getting one, too. Dan chuckled, remembering how disgusted he had been with them, since they hadn't seemed to understand about sudden weddings. Now, he had to admit that maybe it was better that he and Angelica had been forced back into their normal lifestyles. It was an understatement to say that they were busy. More like swamped.

Patrick squirmed around restlessly, and Dan straightened. "I better get back in there before Angelica negotiates the entire company out from under the poor man."

He had insisted that the meetings take place here in their suite at the hotel for Angelica's convenience. It was unorthodox, but it helped to put her at ease. Besides, it wouldn't hurt if he also began acquiring the traditional computer company owner's reputation for eccentricity. What the hell, he thought in amusement. The Apple guys had parlayed it into a multimillion-dollar corporation.

". . . my client requires separate accounting," Angelica was saying as he reentered the room. "We have a very unusual agreement with Starlight Software."

"We read over the agreements you sent to us, and that doesn't pose a problem," Jimenez said. "However, we will want exclusive licensing in the future."

That was a new twist, Dan thought, sitting back down in his chair. They hadn't mentioned exclusive licensing before. It would be good for both Starlight and Diana, since Mark IV had enormous resources worldwide. He glanced at Angelica and nodded slightly.

She smiled at Jimenez. "We're open to a discussion on that. . . ."

When the negotiations finally, and very satisfactorily, ended several hours later, Angelica grinned widely at him.

"That went much better than I thought it would," she said, collapsing back into her chair.

"I told you it would," he said, sitting down opposite her on the sofa. He picked up Patrick from the rockerseat. The baby had awakened from his nap just in time for the last of the wheeling-dealing.

"Of course you did," she said. "And next time I promise to get a baby-sitter. I'm still nervous about leaving Patrick."

Her tone was a little too conciliatory, and Dan frowned. She had promised to give the marriage a chance, but sometimes she seemed to be biting back her words. Like now.

"Well, I suppose we're going to have to start looking for a house here in the city," she said, glancing around the suite. "We've got an extra five minutes now that the negotiations are just about settled."

He chuckled. "Five is about it. Let's let it go for a while. After all, we're barely settled."

"But . . . of course." She smiled brightly. "You're absolutely right."

He sighed with exasperation. "Angelica, quit being so damn agreeable."

"I am being agreeable to help us have a normal marriage," she said, in a schoolteacher voice.

"I understand that," he said. "But I don't want that. That's not really giving it a true chance."

"Fine. I think we ought to go house hunting right away." She blinked. "Lord, but that felt good."

"And it sounded good."

She grinned at him. "But we still have a problem. I want to call a realtor now, and you want to wait."

"So we negotiate a settlement. Let's call this weekend."

"Great." She laughed. "And I do mean it."

"See, that wasn't so bad."

She made a face at him, then stood up. "I think I'll change out of this thing and go shopping, since you're here." She flapped the bottom of her long tailored jacket. Combined with her modest skirt and silk blouse, it was a very professional-looking outfit. "I need more clothes."

"Patrick and I will go with you."

"Oh, no, you won't," she said tartly. "I also need some peace and quiet."

"In a department store?"

"I've discovered that I have to take it where I can get it. Besides, I'm entitled to a reward after today. And that means leaving you two hooligans at home."

Dan smiled as he watched her leave the room. She was relaxing, and he was inordinately pleased about that. Actually, he thought, the marriage was going very well—especially at night. She might not be initiating their lovemaking, but she was a willing participant. In a way, they were still circling each other cautiously. He had a good idea that wouldn't pose a problem for too much longer. But he was through rushing their relationship.

The telephone rang, and he groaned. He was too comfortable to get up and answer it. Besides, Patrick was happily trying to eat his tie, and he didn't have the heart to shift him. Angelica, however, came to the rescue.

"I'll get it," she called from the bedroom.

"You're a wonderful woman," he called back.

She made a rude comment which he chose to ignore. Instead, he stretched out on the sofa and settled the baby on his chest. Finally and at last, things seemed to be smoothing out, he thought contentedly, and closed his eyes.

"I saw ya on the TV with my kid."

Angelica's stomach lurched at the words spoken by the hard young female voice on the other end of the line.

"Who is this?" she asked numbly.

"Who do you think?"

Angelica tried to calm her racing heart. "What do you want?"

"Well, I been thinkin' that you sure did look happy with the kid. You and that rich guy you married. You're rich, too, aren't ya?"

Angelica didn't bother to correct the girl.

"People didn't like it that you two weren't married before. But ya got married, didn't ya? I think you and I should have a chat about that."

Angelica knew she should encourage the girl to call the authorities. She knew that if she couldn't talk the girl into that, she should report this conversation herself.

"I agree," she said, deciding a little chat alone *first* wouldn't hurt. "If you would like to come here—"

"No!" She clearly heard the panic in the girl's voice. "No, you meet me at Pioneer Square, in front of the Bay Café. And the talk is just between you and me, lady. You got that?"

Angelica drew in a deep breath. "Yes."

"Good. Be there in fifteen minutes."

The phone clicked dead before she could say anything. She hung up the receiver and stood still for a moment. Time was precious, but she'd waste more if she panicked. She would be better off if she pulled herself together first.

Dammit, she thought angrily. Why now? Why did Patrick's mother have to show up at all? She knew she had to tell Dan, and she slowly walked into the sitting room.

Her heart turned over when she saw him dozing on the sofa, little Patrick snuggled against him. The baby was contentedly sucking on his thumb while his other hand explored Dan's nose and mouth.

In that instant, she realized she was in love with Dan. She had tried too hard to convince herself that she wasn't, and she'd nearly succeeded. It was all so clear to her now why she had married him, in spite of her doubts and insecurities. Dan was a part of her. The most important part. She had fought and argued and married and made love with him, and she'd done it for the sake of love.

And then there was Patrick. She didn't know what his mother wanted, but she would damn well find out, she thought. She couldn't let anything come between the three of them again. They were a family now. The thing she had been so afraid of had finally happened, and she admitted that she was relieved that it had. She had always preferred her crises to be up-front.

She walked over to the sofa and bent down to kiss Patrick. The baby raised his head and grinned sloppily at her. A fierce possessiveness shot through her, and she kissed the beloved funny little face again.

She knelt down next to Dan and opened her mouth to tell him of the phone call . . . and stopped herself. The girl had made it clear that only she should come. She wouldn't be expecting Dan. Angelica knew that if she told Dan he would insist on coming, and if he did, the girl might panic and run. The worst part was, they wouldn't even know it. She couldn't let that happen.

Pushing the hair off his brow, she whispered, "Danny, I'm going now."

He blinked once, then opened his eyes. "Okay. Bring back something sexy."

"For me or for you?" she asked softly.

He came fully awake at the teasing remark. Gazing at her, he asked, "Are you being provocative?"

"Yes," she said firmly. "And if you're lucky, I'll seduce you later."

"I will be damned," he said breathily and in awe.

"You will be loved."

She rose to her feet and walked out the door.

Ten

Angelica assessed the young woman sitting across the small table from her, and readily admitted she didn't care for what she could see. The girl was in her early twenties and blowsy, and her jeans and zippered sweatsuit jacket needed contact with soap and water. It wasn't that so much, Angelica thought. It was the uncaring hardness in the girl's eyes that infuriated her beyond reason.

The girl drank her soda and chewed on the ice. Angelica left her coffee untouched in front of her. Her mind twisted away from the thought of sharing something as normal as a drink with the girl.

She had given her name as Jane Smith. Angelica knew it wasn't her real one. And that was fine. Angelica didn't want to know anything about the woman that she would have to connect with Patrick. She didn't want Patrick to be a part of this person.

Her only consolation was that Patrick held no physical trace of the dark-haired, sallow-skinned Jane Smith.

"How could you leave Patrick like that?" she asked, remembering the baby on the bed unprotected from rolling off. She had never quite been able to believe that anyone would callously dump a child, especially one like Patrick.

The girl laughed. "Is that what you call him? Mar—I called him Jimmy."

Angelica hated the name instantly. Her anger at the girl's attitude was mounting with each moment. She wanted to slap Jane Smith. Instead, she forced her shaking hands to remain still on her lap. She was dimly aware of people laughing and chatting at the other tables of the Bay Café, and the normal behavior grated on her nerves.

"Why did you abandon your child?" she asked coldly. "A tiny baby left—"

"I—I had to! I couldn't take care of him no more. I was scared to keep him. It was so hard to feed him. . . ."

The girl's voice was becoming more and more whiny and ingratiating.

"I see." Angelica eyed her suspiciously at the sudden change in personality. "Maybe you better tell me why you asked me to meet you."

The girl now looked confused, as if Angelica had asked her to jump off a cliff. At least, Angelica thought with relief, the girl was still in her chair. She'd almost lost her temper, and that might have chased Jane Smith away.

The girl seemed to come to some inner decision and relaxed again.

"Well . . . see . . . I see ya on the news, talking about the baby and stuff, and sayin' that you were taking care of him. You really love him, don't ya?"

"Yes," Angelica said, easily sensing where the girl was headed. After all, she was hardly being subtle.

"Well, I want you to have him, see? I think that would be real nice. But you can't have him unless I say you can, right?"

Here it comes, Angelica thought with growing disgust.

"Like, so, maybe we could arrange something, maybe . . ."

"Yes?" she prompted, when the girl hesitated.

"Well, see, I do wanna sign papers or whatever saying I give the kid to you."

"A private adoption."

"Yeah, right," the girl said brightly. "A private adoption. I mean, I have bills and stuff from when I had him. Babies cost lots, so I'm gonna need money. . . ."

"I see," Angelica said. She saw all too well. The girl wanted money for Patrick. Anger, pure and hot, poured through her at the thought, and yet she wasn't at all surprised. Calmly, she said, "I'm afraid there are complications to doing that, since Patrick has been made a ward of the state."

"But . . ." The girl looked flummoxed. "But, he's my kid."

"That's debatable," Angelica muttered.

"What?"

She cleared her throat. "The state has custody of Patrick now. If you want the child back—"

"But I don't want him!" the girl exclaimed.

Angelica tried not to let her vast relief show. That had been a fear she hadn't dared to acknowledge. "The point is that you will have to sign away any rights to the baby with the state. They, in turn, will make him available for adoption. And then my husband and I can apply for him."

"But I left him at the hotel!" The girl looked ready to bolt out of her chair, as she glanced wildly around the café. "I heard about your . . . husband, that he was rich, so I left Jimmy in his room. If I wanted the . . . state, I woulda gave the baby to them!"

Heads turned toward them in curiosity, and Angelica rushed in. "I understand that, Ms. Smith. Really, I do. And I'm trying to help you. But a private adoption isn't possible now. I'm also a lawyer, and I know this. You really do need to get in touch with the State Social and—"

"No!" the girl nearly shrieked. "I can't do none of this state stuff."

Angelica began again. "I know you're scared. But they'll understand that you're young, and you were unsure of how to proceed about giving up a baby. It's happened before. My friend Martha will help you and . . . the baby. But if you truly want him to go to a good home, then you're going to have to legally give him up. And you can't do that unless you get in touch with the authorities."

"No!" The girl's eyes were almost wild with fear.

"Okay," Angelica said soothingly, terrified the girl would break for the door. "It's okay. I really want to help you . . . Jane. You say you want to give Patrick to us, and we want him. But you need to understand what's involved here."

The girl sat warily on the edge of her chair. "I'm not going to no State Social and . . . and—"

"Health Services." Angelica stared at the girl. "Then I don't know how you can help the baby."

"Can't I just sign a paper or something now that says I give the child to you?" the girl asked.

Angelica carefully began to frame an answer. "With the state involved—"

To her complete astonishment, the girl suddenly scrambled out of the chair and ran for the door.

"Wait!" she shouted, jumping up and running after her. "Dammit, wait a minute!"

A couple came into the café just as the girl reached the door. Angelica cried out in frustration as Jane Smith ducked around the couple and out of the café.

"Why didn't you stop her?" she demanded, while playing bob-and-weave as the couple and she tried to sidestep each other.

"What?"

She raced outside the café precious seconds later only to find the girl had disappeared into the heavy flow of shoppers and tourists. Cursing fervently, she spun around in a circle, her gaze searching the crowd. No running form caught her eye.

She had lost "Jane Smith."

"Damn, damn, damn!" she exclaimed, balling her hands into fists.

She had pushed too hard, she berated herself. She'd thought she could talk to the girl, and she had been wrong. Worse, she could easily imagine what Martha Canfield would have to say about this disaster. Then she imagined what Dan would have to say. Then she groaned aloud.

"She asked only for me, Dan. . . ."

Dan listened to Angelica explain her little shopping trip detour with an outward calmness that surprised him. The anger inside him felt ready to erupt at any second.

". . . Besides, I didn't want to involve you since I should have reported the contact right away to Martha."

"That's no excuse for not telling me," he said, glowering at her.

"Yes, it is," she said, glowering back. She was holding Patrick strategically in front of her. "It was enough for me to take the chance. You know you would have insisted on going. And that would have scared the girl away, so what good would it have done to tell you?"

He wondered if she were right, then decided it was still no excuse. She should have told him about the phone call from Patrick's mother. It had been foolish of her to keep it from him. Fear surfaced in his mind. Anything could have happened to her, and nobody would have known where she was.

"You should have told me," he said. They were the only words he could get out at the moment.

"You would have insisted on going!" she repeated. "I couldn't trust you not to."

Pain, deep and wounding, knifed through his body. He suddenly realized that was the real heart of the matter. Despite all they had shared, she couldn't trust him. She hadn't trusted him *again*. Nothing had changed between them. He thought about the words she had said right before she left. They had been a lie to soothe and mislead him from seeing or sensing something was up with her.

He turned away from her abruptly and walked over to one of the sitting room chairs. He sat down heavily on it.

"Dan, please try to understand," she said, following him. "I didn't want you to get into trouble."

"You still don't understand about trust, do you?" he asked. "I thought you were going to give this marriage a chance."

"I was!" she nearly shouted. "I was giving it the best chance—"

"No," he broke in, before she could say more. "It's exactly what you were *not* doing. Giving it a chance means sharing. You don't know how to share. You didn't even consider that this was information I was entitled to know."

"Dammit! Will you listen? This had nothing to do with trusting you."

"It has everything to do with it."

"Danny, Patrick's mot—Jane Smith said only I

could meet her! She probably would have taken off if she'd seen you with me."

"That is not the point here," he said harshly.

"Are you telling me that you wouldn't have insisted on going?"

"I . . ." He stared at her for a long moment. "I truthfully don't know, but—"

"See?" she cried triumphantly.

"I was going to add that I wasn't given the chance to find out."

She gazed at him mutely.

"I wasn't given the chance," he repeated numbly. "You never gave anything between us a chance."

"No," she whispered, then added more forcefully, "No. Dan, don't you understand? As a lawyer, I'm an officer of the court, and I couldn't involve you in any trouble that might come out of this for me. And, dammit, the girl was expecting only me! Anyone else would have scared her away."

"You said she saw the television interview," he reminded her. "She would have known who I was—if I had gone with you."

"Dan, I trust you. Please understand—"

"Oh, I understand all right."

"No, you don't. I wanted to help get Patrick free. For you."

He closed his eyes. It was just like her to have a noble reason on top of everything else, he thought. But the truth, no matter how it was wrapped, was still the truth. She hadn't trusted him. Without trust, how could they have a marriage? How could they have anything?

He stood up. "I've got some work to do."
He went into the bedroom and shut the door.

Angelica sat on the bed in her old room in the suite and stared at the wall. Patrick had been put to bed for the night, blissfully unaware of the turmoil brewing between his guardians. Dan had again retreated to his suite, the door shut.

She admitted to herself she was afraid to invade his privacy. She had been sharing his bed, giving the marriage a "chance," but he'd made it clear he didn't want her anymore. She was so fragile now, she couldn't open that door and face a physical rejection too. She'd break into a thousand pieces.

None of her reasons for excluding him mattered really, she thought, closing her eyes in pain. What mattered was that she had hurt Dan, and she wished with all her heart she could take it back. But how? Meeting with that girl had had nothing to do with trust or the lack of it.

But he saw it that way, and she had no idea how to correct his notion. Clearly, his idea of trust was quite different from her own.

She had been deluding herself, she thought. She and Dan weren't any closer to agreeing on fundamentals than they had ever been. She had allowed herself to be swept away by . . . love. She had known better, but despite all her fears, it had happened anyway. She had fallen in love, and now it was turning on her. "Killing her softly," she thought. Funny how apt that song title was.

She had no one to blame but herself. She'd gone into this, if reluctantly, with her eyes wide open. Now it was falling apart, just as she'd been afraid it would.

Realizing she'd been sitting there on the bed for a long time, she finally forced herself to get up. She walked quietly into the baby's room, glanced once at the closed door to the other bedroom, and sat down on the sofa. She watched Patrick suck on his thumb as he slept. Her heart flipped over . . . and she realized who really had been hurt by today's fiasco with Jane Smith.

"What else was I supposed to do, Patrick?" she whispered.

The baby moved slightly and smiled around his thumb, as if to say he understood she had done her best for him and he forgave her anyway.

The door to the other suite opened, startling her out of her thoughts.

"Is something wrong with Patrick?" Dan asked. He was standing in the doorway, dressed in his robe.

She drew in a deep breath, acutely conscious of her own thin cotton nightgown and matching robe. "No. I . . . just thought I'd sit with him for a while."

He turned away and stared at the baby. "It's very late."

She glanced at her watch and noted it was after two. "Yes. Were you working?"

He hesitated for a moment, then nodded. "I had some catching up to do."

"It piles up, doesn't it?" she said, gazing at him.

"Yes."

They had been whispering so as not to disturb the baby. Despite the courtesy, Patrick blinked sleepily and opened his eyes. He stared at her unwinkingly, still sucking on his thumb.

"I suppose you want a bottle," she said to the infant.

"He's about due anyway," Dan said, stepping fully into the room. "I'll get it."

"Thank you," she murmured, hating the stilted conversation between them. Even in the beginning, she doubted if they had been so stiff with each other.

She changed Patrick's diaper with absentminded expertise, as she thought about how painfully politely she and Dan were acting. She wished desperately for a fight, but the spark of anger was gone completely. What had happened earlier showed how . . . unsuitable they were for each other, she finally realized. Opposites might attract, but that was hardly the foundation for a solid commitment.

"I'll feed him," Dan said as he returned from the kitchenette.

She nodded and handed the baby over to him. Awkwardly, she perched on the arm of the sofa and watched, not wanting to leave yet.

"What was she like?" Dan suddenly asked.

"Hard. Streetwise and greedy. I'm sorry I lost her."

He raised his eyebrows.

"I *am* sorry. I didn't know what else to do, Dan."

He was silent for a moment. "Forget it."

He turned away, and she felt the rejection as sharply as if he had said it. She closed her eyes. Nothing in her life had ever been as painful as this moment.

"Since you have him," she finally said, opening her eyes, "I'll go to bed then."

She got up and walked toward her old bedroom.

He didn't stop her.

Eleven

"So you went to meet the girl yesterday. Without telling me."

Angelica grimaced as she heard the exasperation in Martha's voice clearly through the telephone line. It seemed she wouldn't get past this point in the story *again*. "I'm telling you now, Martha."

"You're a tad late, aren't you?" Martha boomed.

"Yes." Angelica readjusted the receiver at her ear and sighed. "She asked me to meet her, and she made it clear I was to come alone. I don't think she would have talked to anybody else."

"Well . . . that did put you in a bind, I admit."

"Yes. Dan knew absolutely nothing about it. I felt I had to do as she asked."

"I see. I don't suppose there was much else you could do. . . ."

Angelica stiffled a bitter laugh at Martha's words.

She would have been much happier if another person had understood.

". . . But you should have reported the meeting to me first thing *afterward*."

"Yes, I know." Angelica was silent for a moment. "I'm sorry. I . . . Dan wasn't too happy with me when I told him, and to be truthful I forgot about you."

"Gave you hell, did he?"

If only it were just that, Angelica thought, briefly closing her eyes. "Yes. He gave me hell."

Martha was quiet for a moment, and Angelica wondered if the other woman realized there was more to the "hell" than just angry words and would drop the subject. She hoped so, since she was in no mood to explain.

"Did you get any information from the girl?" Martha asked at last. "Who she was? Where she lives? Anything?"

"Not much." She stared at Patrick as he lay in his crib and tried to catch his Winnie-the-Pooh mobile. Piglet kept spinning out of reach. "She claimed her name was Jane Smith, no address. She wanted money for Patrick. For a private adoption."

"I hope to hell you didn't give her any," Martha said sternly.

"Of course not. I know better than that. I tried to get her to call you. She got scared, and I didn't want to press her too much, but she took off anyway. I don't think I handled it well."

"You probably did," Martha said. "It's obvious that it was a deliberate abandonment of her baby, and she was compounding that by trying to extort money. The last person she would want to talk to is me. It's no wonder she got scared. However, she sounds like an opportunist."

"She seemed that way," Angelica said. "I couldn't believe her callousness over Patrick."

"There're all kinds in the world, and I've seen most. At least you can give me a description of her, and we do know that she was in the city as of yesterday. She might call again, and if she does, this time you call me right away. We'll decide then how to handle a meeting. We're very flexible about this kind of thing."

"You've done it before?" Angelica asked.

"I told you, we're not bureaucratic ogres."

"You mean *you're* not."

Martha chuckled. "I'm notorious for bending rules."

When Angelica finally hung up the phone, she was able to smile slightly. It was a relief, she thought, to truly talk to someone about yesterday's disastrous meeting. And to hear someone understand—just a little. She didn't feel she had made too many mistakes.

A tiny voice reminded her that Martha was not exactly the same as Dan. And yet she couldn't help feeling that Dan should have understood her dilemma. But he hadn't. In bewilderment, she could only wonder why. . . .

"No more," she said out loud, getting up off the sofa.

He had let her go last night, just let her walk into her old bedroom without a word. She had shut the door and heard finality in the quiet click of the lock.

The pain had been blinding, but she had refused to give in to tears. This morning when Patrick's cries had awakened her from her semiconsciousness, she felt as if she had a tremendous hangover.

Four aspirin later, she didn't feel that much better. The awkwardness between her and Dan had been worse with the daylight. Even Patrick had finally sensed something was wrong between his adults, and he'd been fussy that morning until after Dan had left for the office.

It only confirmed what she had realized last night. She and Dan were on too entirely different levels emotionally to have a workable marriage. In fact, yesterday was only the latest example of their basic lack of understanding. And the more they stayed together the worse things would get.

Yet none of that had stopped her from falling in love with him, she thought. It was ironic to realize that *the* man was the wrong man. Everything between them had been unique . . . and totally wrong. She had fought her attraction for so long and succumbed anyway. The pain she was feeling now was well deserved for the mess she had created.

Sadly, she watched the baby frown, then begin to fuss as he became bored with the mobile game. She stood up and went over to the crib. Lifting Patrick up, she cuddled the little sweetly-soft body to her breast. A wave of love swept over her as he tucked his head naturally onto her shoulder.

"You certainly know how to complicate things, bunny," she whispered, her heart telling her what she would have to do.

Dan wanted this child so much, she thought. One day soon Patrick would be free for adoption . . . and she loved Dan enough to step away when that time came. Tonight, she would tell him that. It would be so hard to let them both go . . . yet she could do it, she told herself, swallowing back her tears. Because she loved them.

And because it was the right thing to do.

"Yes, Mike. I'll tell her. She'll be pleased."

Dan closed his eyes as he held the telephone receiver to his ear and listened helplessly to Mike Jimenez go on and on about Angelica's charm. Just what he didn't need right now, he thought. From the moment her door had closed last night, he had wished he'd called her back. . . .

". . . And you two certainly make a good team," Jimenez continued. "You three, I should say. You've got yourself a cute little guy there."

Dan shifted restlessly in his chair. "I know."

"I've never been to a negotiation with a baby before. You know, you and Angelica have to be one of the most extraordinary business stories—"

"Mike, what about the programmers?" he interrupted, wishing he had never called the man on several contract details.

"The programmers? Oh, they'll be sending up those changes for your people to see."

"Diana will have to see them, too," Dan reminded him.

"Of course. After all, it's a courtesy to run them by the game's inventor."

Dan was about to make a comment when his intercom buzzed. Surprised that his secretary would interrupt him on an important phone call, he hesitated for a moment, then said, "Hang on a minute, Mike."

"Sure, sure."

He put Mike on hold and pressed the winking button.

His secretary instantly said, "I'm sorry, but a girl is insisting that she talk to you about the baby. She sounds . . . not like a nut. I don't know. I wasn't sure what to do. . . ."

"It's not Angelica?" he asked, his stomach starting to churn as he wondered frantically if something were wrong with Patrick.

"No, sir. A Jane Smith."

The name was a shock of lightning bolting through him, freezing him to the spot.

"I'll take it," he forced himself to say. "Tell Mike Jimenez something has come up, and I'll get back to him."

"Right."

He pressed another button and a young female voice came on the line. "Took your stupid secretary long enough."

At the hard brash tone, Dan was instantly reminded of Angelica's description of the girl. Suddenly, he realized he had no idea what had been said between this girl and Angelica. Dammit, he thought. He'd been too angry even to ask.

"Can I help you?" he said neutrally.

"Well, now. I was talking to your wife yesterday . . . about my baby. I guess you know that."

He could feel the hairs on his neck rise instantly. "Yes, I'm aware of the meeting."

"Well, I kinda got scared the way she kept talkin' about my having to sign the papers from the state. I couldn't take care of my baby no more, see? So I tried to give him a good home, but I didn't know things would get all messed up. . . ."

Her voice trailed off, and Dan frantically wondered where the girl was heading.

"See, I wanna do what's right for my baby, like I told your wife. About signing those papers from the state to make it legal and all. Well, I wanna do that now. But babies . . . they cost a lot. I . . . if I just sign the papers . . . well, I'm not gonna get any money, am I? The state isn't gonna pay me nothing. I gave him to you, ya know. I wanted you to have him."

"I understand completely," Dan said, forcibly holding back his anger.

"I thought so. I'll be glad to sign those papers . . . after. See, I really need a lot—"

"How much?" he interrupted, gripping the receiver tightly.

"Do I need?"

"Yes."

"$10,000."

The creature was incredible, he thought numbly. Streetwise and greedy, Angelica had said. And knowing when to bargain hard, he added.

"Now you see why I can't sign unless I have some money. Do ya think you can help me out?"

"I think I might," he said, his mind racing.

"Now that's real nice of you," Jane Smith said. "I thought you and I would get along. I really want to do the right thing, like I said. And I really do want to sign those papers, like I said. But I need the money first."

"Yes." She kept mentioning papers, he thought, so he asked, "Shall I bring the papers?"

"Your wife said I had to see some lady and sign them!" the girl exclaimed. "Now you're saying I can—"

"My wife is a lawyer," he broke in, hearing the anger and panic in her voice. Wrong move, he thought wildly. "If she said you have to see someone, then you must have to. She would know. I really don't."

He heard the girl mutter a vulgar curse, then she said, "Well, okay. But I'm not signing anything until I get that money. You come this time and alone. You bring anybody and I won't be there."

"How will I know you?"

"I'll know you," the girl said. "Just stand under the Third Avenue exit sign at King Street Station. Two hours is enough time for a rich guy like you to get the money."

"Yes—"

"Two hours." The phone clicked off abruptly.

Two hours later, Dan stood impatiently underneath the Third Avenue exit sign. In his breast pocket was an envelope filled with a special kind of money. Traceable money.

Not quite what the girl had wanted, he mused, studiously ignoring the young man bouncing happily by with his blaring portable radio. The punk music was loud and very natural, he thought gratefully, as the young man stopped a short distance away. He only hoped the girl thought so too. From his position against the wall under the Third Avenue sign, Dan watched people of all shapes and sizes flow in and out of the station. His muscles tightened at the sight of every young woman. He'd been here for a few minutes and none had stopped so far.

He had been forced to recognize the dilemma Angelica had faced yesterday, when the girl had requested to meet her alone. He had been hurt that she hadn't told him, and he'd been scared, too, that she might have run into trouble, but she'd had very little choice. None, really. It had taken a tremendous effort for him *not* to follow the girl's instructions to the letter, he admitted ruefully. In fact, he had wasted quite a few minutes arguing himself into informing Martha of the latest phone call. Things had moved swiftly after that, fortunately. Even now, seeing the young officer he had spoken with earlier playing his part to perfection did little to relieve the anxiety skittering along his nerves. The truth was, he felt as if he had made a horrible mistake by calling in the authorities. He could easily understand now that Angelica had done what she thought was best, and he could no longer fault her.

He owed her one large apology. He had known it last night, when he had gone to bed with just his pride. The only person who didn't understand trust was himself. He hoped he could repair the damage with her when he got home.

He cleared his throat nervously and adjusted his

glasses, wondering what she would say when she found out where he had been. There hadn't been time to call her and tell her the latest news. Oh, well, he thought, in dry amusement. It would be her turn to freeze him out. But only for a—

"You're Roberts."

The voice that startled him out of his thoughts was the one that had been etched in his brain two hours ago. Attached to it was a dark-haired girl in a cheap scrubby jacket and jeans. Her eyes were hard and wary.

"Yes," he said, staring at her and trying to memorize her features. If anything went wrong . . .

"I'm Jane Smith. You got the money?"

He nodded and reached into the breast pocket of his suit. He removed the envelope and tried not to look beyond the girl to the man with the radio. He handed it to her.

She seemed ready to dart away at the least movement, but she did open the envelope's flap and glance inside.

"It all better be here," she said harshly.

"It is," he assured her. He frantically tried to keep her talking to signal to the police that this was the girl. "Will you go to State Social and Health Services now and sign the papers?"

The girl smiled and stuffed the envelope into the waistband of her jeans. The man with the radio was moving toward them, finally. But he seemed to be in slow motion. In horror, Dan realized the girl was calmly walking away from him as if she'd never stopped in the first place. Another few steps and she would melt into the crowd.

He reached out automatically and grabbed her wrist tightly. He could feel her bones under her skin. The girl squawked once, then everyone around them seemed to explode into action. Before he could blink, people were shoving him away into the wall and spinning the girl around. Handcuffs were clamped on her wrists and her rights were being read to her.

Dan shook his head to clear it and straightened away from the wall. A tall black woman, dressed conspicuously in a leopard skirt and purple tights, was already leading Jane Smith away. A "bum" and the young man with the radio followed behind. Jane Smith suddenly jerked away from the policewoman and turned around. She glared at him for a long moment.

And then she laughed triumphantly.

The hairs on Dan's neck rose and some instinct inside him instantly knew something was very wrong. A vision of Angelica and Patrick alone and unprotected raced through his mind.

He uttered a barnyard curse and ran for his car.

As the gray sky deteriorated into late afternoon drizzle, Angelica walked away from her suite window with Patrick in her arms. She had been showing him Mount Rainier. Not that Patrick noticed the extinct volcano as much as he did the raindrops coursing down the window, she thought. Still, the view was stunning from twenty stories up.

"Wait until the fall," she said to the baby. "Then you can watch it rain every day until summer comes again. You'll like trying to catch the raindrops."

As she set the infant into his rockerseat, she wondered if Dan would be working late at Starlight tonight. She wondered if he would even call her to tell her that.

If he didn't, then she would call him. She'd go down there. She had to get her decision out before she exploded with it. Her musings were interrupted when she heard a faint knocking on Dan's suite door.

"Don't bother to get up, Patrick," she said, buckling the seat strap. "I'll just answer that, shall I?"

She walked through Dan's bedroom, trying not to glance at the bed they had shared, and on into the other sitting room. The knock came again, louder this time.

"Yes?"

"Room service," a muffled voice called through the door.

"Room service?" she muttered in puzzlement. She opened the door to find a red-jacketed waiter standing behind a linen-covered table. "I didn't—"

That was as far as she got. The waiter shoved the table straight into her, and she was knocked off her feet. She landed with a hard thump on the floor as the table careened wildly past her. She gasped for breath in speechless shock.

"Where's the damn kid?" the man shouted at her as he darted around the room. "Where the hell's that kid!"

Angelica understood two things at once. That the waiter was no waiter, and that he wanted Patrick. Overwhelming fear shot through her, and then she realized that the man had no idea where Patrick was . . . for the moment.

Galvanized into action, she scrambled to her feet, just as the man started toward the open bedroom door.

"No!" she screamed, grabbing up a vase. She threw it at him and, to her horror, missed.

The man turned around in complete astonishment as the vase sailed past him before smashing into the wall. "What the hell—?"

Angelica literally launched herself into the air, as the maternal urge to protect rose to a peak within her. She slammed into the man, and they both went down in a tangle of arms and legs. She quickly sorted herself out, and sitting atop his chest, swung her fists wildly and continually, hitting anything and anywhere she could. The man yelled and tried to fend her off. From somewhere deep inside her she found the strength to avoid his stronger hands and keep pummeling. She heard his pleas for release, and ignored them with a primitive satisfaction. Her brain chanted over and over, "You won't touch my baby."

Hands, too many to fight, were suddenly pulling her off the waiter. Her arms were pinned to her body. She screamed in vindictive fear that he was being rescued and Patrick would be taken from her.

"Angelica! Angelica!"

She struggled to break free from the person holding her so tightly.

"We got him, Angelica. It's okay, sweetheart. It's okay. You're safe. He won't touch you again."

The red haze cleared, and she became aware that it was Dan speaking to her, holding her. She stopped her wild movements. It filtered into her brain that the room was filled with people in organized chaos. Excited voices reached her returning senses.

"Hotel security . . . Detective Marshall . . . I think she was trying to kill me. . . . Yeah, yeah, he's breaking my heart, Ralph. . . . We got your girlfriend. . . . He used to work here. . . . Get up, creep."

"Angelica, are you okay?" Dan asked, tilting her head up.

She nodded shakily. "I told you room service isn't all it's cracked up to be."

"I think you're right," he said, his eyes searching hers as he held her even more tightly to him.

She swallowed back a sudden rush of tears and wrapped her arms around his neck. Their mouths fused together frantically. The fear faded, and she felt safe and protected and comforted . . . and wanted. How much she needed Dan's arms around her right now, she thought. And how much she needed to be kissed like this . . . as if she were the one woman on the earth for him.

Suddenly she remembered Patrick, and she instantly broke away from Dan.

"Patrick!"

Dan cursed, and the two of them raced into the other room. Patrick, still strapped into his rockerseat, looked up at them and smiled angelically. He had somehow managed to pull some papers off the coffee table and had happily mouthed and crumpled them into a wet accordion.

Angelica breathed a sigh of relief, as tears dripped down her cheeks.

"You little stinker," she said happily. "That's my only copy of the Mark IV contract."

Dan laughed.

"Thank goodness, Jane Smith wasn't really Patrick's mother," Angelica said. "Hand me a sleeper."

Dan acknowledged with a nod that he couldn't have agreed more with her. "Mickey Mouse or Pound Puppy?" he asked.

"Pound Puppy."

He dug out the appropriate sleeper from the back of the changer shelf and gave it to her. He had other, more important things to discuss, but he was waiting impatiently until they were finally alone.

"Still," he said, deciding to pick up on her comment about Jane Smith, "she and her ex-hotel waiter boyfriend did put Patrick in my bedroom that day. I suppose we should thank them for that."

The pair had confessed to the police that they had abandoned Patrick. The boyfriend had been fired from the hotel recently, and they had thought it a kick to dump the baby on the "rich bachelor" in the top-floor suite. It wasn't until they had seen all the publicity about his and Angelica's engagement and marriage that Jane Smith had decided such people might just be willing to pay to keep a baby, especially since they were getting married for it. A pair of amateurs through and through, they had planned to extort money for signing over the baby, then kidnap Patrick back, go elsewhere, and try it again with another wealthy couple. The girl had panicked, and run from Angelica when she'd realized the authorities were already involved. But she'd later decided the plan would still work if she offered to sign the necessary papers after getting the money. She'd thought Dan would be more willing than Angelica to fork over the cash. Jane Smith and her waiter never would have gotten away with it, Dan thought with satisfaction, although Angelica did prove the point pretty thoroughly with the boyfriend. He was the weaker, more nervous of the two, the police said, and he'd given them quite a bit of information.

Including some about Patrick's real mother.

Dan shook his head sadly. She had been a runaway teenager, and ironically in foster homes most of her life. She had lived on the streets before hooking up with Jane Smith and her boyfriend. Dan could only wonder what had driven the girl to them. Maybe she was desperate for a place to have her baby. She'd been too scared to go to a hospital. She had been killed in a car accident a few days before Patrick had suddenly appeared in his room. The other two, of course, hadn't wanted the child and so they had gotten rid of him the easiest way possible.

"Actually they did Patrick a big favor," Dan said, staring down at the baby. "I think his mother would have been . . . pleased."

"I know." Angelica was quiet for a moment. "They said she called him Jimmy. I've tried, but I can't think of him that way. He's been Patrick too long for me."

The baby turned his head at the sound of his name.

"I think he wants it, Angelica," Dan said. "I think he knows somehow that he's starting over."

She smiled. "I like that."

"Martha said that her department can release him now for adoption."

She nodded, almost absently, to his disappointment.

"I keep thinking about her," she said. "The mother, I mean. I get furious and I want to cry for her at the same time over the senselessness of it. She clearly fell through all the cracks in the system. At least her child will have a better life."

Patrick never questioned the special kisses he got that night, or the extra hugs. He simply took them as his rightful due.

When the baby was settled at last in his crib, Dan immediately took Angelica's arm and led her into his bedroom.

"I have to talk to you. I've needed to all day, but we've had too damn many interruptions."

Angelica slipped out of his grasp. She put some distance between them—too much for his liking—before she turned around to face him. "I agree that we have some things to settle."

That sounded ominous to him.

"Maybe I can settle them," he said, hoping to rectify matters between them. "I found out today just how stupid I am about trust. I was completely and totally wrong—"

"I can understand why you were so angry yesterday," she interrupted. "I should have told you. I know I should have done what you did."

"Angelica," he said forcefully. "You did what she told you to do. That was a right decision, too."

"No," she said, shaking her head. "No, you were right. I realized that."

"Dammit!" he exclaimed. "Forget that part. Can you ever forgive me for the way I acted?"

"Lord," she murmured, beginning to smile. "I wish I had a tape of this."

He stood directly in front of her. "The hell with the tape. Can you forgive me?"

"Yes."

"Good. End of argument."

He reached out and touched her arm, loving the feel of her warm, soft skin. He knew he couldn't live without the touch of her each day. He began to bring her closer. . . .

She resisted.

He blinked. "Angelica—"

"I've been giving this marriage some reevaluation."

His stomach tightened at her words.

"Don't leave me," he said.

She gasped. "Dan—"

"I love you. Don't leave me."

"I can't," she murmured brokenly, coming into his arms. "I thought I could. I . . . it would be best. But I can't."

He held her tightly, knowing he had been so close to losing her through his own foolishness. Never again, he thought fiercely. Never again.

"We need some ground rules," she finally said.

He cursed under his breath. His world was definitely back in order. "Ground rules?"

"Yes."

"What kind of ground rules?" he asked warily.

"That we never *not* fight." Her voice caught. "I didn't realize how good and healthy arguing loudly could be—until you went cold on me."

"Me! You went to your. . . ." He snapped his jaw shut for a second, then said, "I agree to shout at the top of my lungs about everything, as long as you agree that we always go to bed together no matter how hurt or angry you are."

"Me!" she squeaked. "But you didn't ask me to come to bed. You let me go! Dammit, Dan, what else was I supposed to do?"

"Come to bed like a proper wife," he said, grinning. "And then I would have acted like a proper husband, and we would have made up and made love. We were both at fault for being so damned stubborn. So from now on we will fight and we will make up and we will above all have a perfectly normal marriage."

She smiled. "I love you, Danny Roberts."

"I love you, too, wife," he whispered. "Can we make love now?"

"Oh, absolutely."

His lips came down on hers in a searing kiss.

Epilogue

"He said 'bird.' "

"He's pointing at the bell."

"No, he's not. His eye are following the bird."

"Bur!"

"See!" Dan said triumphantly, waving a small bird ornament at his two-year-old son. "Patrick said bird."

Angelica stopped sorting through the Christmas decoration boxes for a moment and watched the child gleefully jab his finger at the glass bell hanging on the bottom branch of the Christmas tree. She stared up at her husband from her position on the floor. "Daniel, open your eyes, please. Our son is playing with the bell, therefore he is saying 'bell.' Now quit fooling around and get this tree decorated, otherwise Santa Claus will never get here tonight!"

Dan set the bird ornament on an upper branch

and said, "That's what I get for marrying a lawyer. You'll fight about anything."

"I never fight with you, my love," she said, smiling demurely.

He laughed as he bent down and kissed her. "I love you anyway. Now Patrick will settle the bird or bell question. Hey, buddy, is it 'bird' or 'bell'?"

Patrick smiled happily and said, "Poo."

"We know what that means," Angelica said, laughing as Dan picked up Patrick and raced for the bathroom.

She had just begun to sort through the boxes again when the doorbell rang. She awkwardly pushed herself to her feet, muttering under her breath at her foolishness for kneeling on the floor. No woman should do that in her seventh month, she decided. She also decided that at the rate she and Dan were going they would be lucky to see their bed before five in the morning.

She walked through her cathedral living room toward the double front doors of their suburban Seattle home. It was a shame, she thought, that they hadn't been able to get to the island for Christmas this year. Maybe next year their work would ease up. She hoped.

She opened the front door . . . and froze when she saw Martha Canfield standing on the porch holding the hand of a tiny Eurasian girl, not more than four years old.

"Merry Christmas, Angelica," Martha said jovially.

Angelica's gaze was helplessly locked on the little girl, on the pinched features, the eyes that held a hopeless fear. Her mind raced with implications. Finally she found her voice. "Martha, Merry Christmas. Come in."

"This is Mai," Martha said, entering the house. "She was just found this evening wandering along the pier, and the police caught me at home. Unfortunately, nobody has reported her missing. We need a temporary shelter for her, and I was wondering if you could help me out. . . ."

Oh Lord, Angelica thought, her heart flipping over.

"I promise it will be very temporary," Martha added.

Angelica merely raised her eyebrows. She'd heard that one before. Turning, she smiled at the girl and held out her hand. "I could use some help with the Christmas tree, Mai. And I have some cookies."

The little girl stared dumbly at her, then let go of Martha's hand and took hers. The short fingers wrapped trustingly around her adult ones.

"Thanks, Angelica," Martha said. "I really didn't know what to do."

"Martha Canfield, you know exactly what you're doing."

Martha grinned.

Angelica grinned back, then she thought of Dan. Taking in another child, however temporarily, should be a joint decision. She hadn't consulted him on this.

Then she realized it wouldn't matter. Like her, he would take one look at Mai and remember another child—their son now. Of course, he would make a semblance of anger that she hadn't discussed Mai with him. But once the yelling was done, he'd be in full agreement with her.

"Oh, Danny!" she called out. "There's someone here you should meet."

"Okay!"

A few seconds later he was standing in the living room, staring speechlessly at Mai. His gaze shifted to Martha, then to Angelica. His expression held a wealth of understanding . . . and a hint of anger for his wife. Then his gaze shifted back to Mai . . . and he melted.

"I have some last minute Christmas shopping to do, don't I?" he said.

"Yes," Angelica said, smiling at him. "It's what I love best about you."

He grinned. "I know."

THE EDITOR'S CORNER

Bantam Books has a *very* special treat for you next month—Nora Roberts's most ambitious, most sizzling novel yet . . .

SWEET REVENGE

Heroine Adrianne, the daughter of a fabled Hollywood beauty and an equally fabled Arab playboy, leads a remarkable double life. The paparazzi and the gossip columnists know her as a modern princess, a frivolous socialite flitting from exclusive watering spot to glittering charity ball. No one knows her as The Shadow, the most extraordinary jewel thief of the decade. She hones her skills at larceny as she parties with the superrich, stealing their trinkets and baubles just for practice . . . for she has a secret plan for the ultimate heist—a spectacular plan to even a bitter score. Her secret is her own until Philip Chamberlain enters her life. Once a renowned thief himself, he's now one of Interpol's smartest, toughest cops . . . and he's falling wildly in love with Adrianne!

SWEET REVENGE will be on sale during the beginning of December when your LOVESWEPTs come into the stores. Be sure to ask your bookseller right now to reserve a copy especially for you.

Now to the delectable LOVESWEPTs you can count on to add to your holiday fun . . . and excitement.

Our first love story next month carries a wonderful round number—LOVESWEPT #300! **LONG TIME COMING,** by Sandra Brown, is as thrilling and original as any romance Sandra has ever written. Law Kincaid, the heart-stoppingly handsome astronaut hero, is in a towering rage when he comes storming up Marnie Hibbs's front walk. He thinks she has been sending him blackmail letters claiming he has a teenage son. As aghast as she is, and still wildly attracted to Law, whom she met seventeen years before when she was just a teen, Marnie tries to put him off and hold her secret close. But the golden and glorious man is determined to wrest the truth from her at any cost! A beautiful love story!

(continued)

Welcome back Peggy Webb, author of LOVESWEPT #301, **HALLIE'S DESTINY,** a marvelous love story featuring a gorgeous "gypsy" whom you met in previous books, Hallie Donovan. A rodeo queen with a heart as big as Texas, Hallie was the woman Josh Butler wanted—he knew it the second he set eyes on her! Josh was well aware of the havoc a bewitching woman like Hallie could wreak in a man's life, but he couldn't resist her. When Josh raked her with his sexy golden eyes and took her captive on a carpet of flowers, Hallie felt a miraculous joy . . . and a great fear, for Josh couldn't—wouldn't—share his life and its problems with her. He sets limits on their love that drive Hallie away . . . until neither can endure without the other. A thrilling romance!

New author Gail Douglas scores another winner with **FLIRTING WITH DANGER,** LOVESWEPT #302. Cassie Walters is a spunky and gorgeous lady who falls under the spell of Bret Parker, a self-made man who is as rich as he is sexy . . . and utterly relentless when it comes to pursuing Cassie. Bret's not quite the womanizer the press made him out to be, as Cassie quickly learns. (I think you'll relish as much as I did the scene in which Michael and Cassie see each other for the first time. Never has an author done more for baby powder and diapers than Gail does in that encounter!) Cassie is terrified of putting down roots . . . and Bret is quite a family man. He has to prove to the woman with whom he's fallen crazily in love that she is brave enough to share his life. A real charmer of a love story crackling with excitement!

In **MANHUNT,** LOVESWEPT #303, Janet Evanovich has created two delightfully adorable and lusty protagonists in a setting that is fascinating. Alexandra Scott—fed up with her yuppie life-style and yearning for a husband and family—has chucked it all and moved to the Alaskan wilderness. She hasn't chosen her new home in a casual way; she's done it using statistics—in Alaska men outnumber women four to one. And right off the bat she meets a man who's one in a million, a dizzyingly attractive avowed bachelor, Michael Casey. But Alex can't be rational about Michael; she loses her head, right along with her heart to him. And to capture him she has to be shameless in her seduction. . . . A true delight!

Get ready to be transported into the heart of a small Southern town and have your funny bone tickled while your
(continued)

heart is warmed when you read **RUMOR HAS IT**, LOVE-SWEPT #304, by Tami Hoag. The outrageous gossip that spreads about Nick Leone when he comes to town to open a restaurant has Katie Quaid as curious as every other woman in the vicinity. She's known as an ice princess, but the moment she and Nick get together she's melting for him. You may shed a tear for Katie—she's had unbearable tragedy in her young life—and you'll certainly gasp with her when Nick presents her with a shocking surprise. A wonderfully fresh and emotionally moving love story!

That marvelous Nick Capoletti you met in Joan Elliott Pickart's last two romances gets his own true love in **SERENITY COVE**, LOVESWEPT #305. When Pippa Pauling discovered Nick Capoletti asleep on the floor of the cabin he'd rented in her cozy mountain lake resort, she felt light-headed with longing and tempted beyond resistance. From the second they first touched, Nick knew Pippa was hearth and home and everything he wanted in life. But Pippa feared that the magic they wove was fleeting. No one could fall in love so fast and make it real for a lifetime. But leave it to Capoletti! In a thrilling climax that takes Pippa and Nick back to Miracles Casino in Las Vegas and the gang there, Pippa learns she can indeed find forever in Nick's arms. A scorching and touching romance from our own Joan Elliott Pickart!

Also in Bantam's general list next month is a marvelous mainstream book that features love, murder, and shocking secrets—**MIDNIGHT SINS**, by new author Ellin Hall. This is a fast-paced and thrilling book with an unforgettable heroine. Don't miss it.

Have a wonderful holiday season.

Carolyn Nichols

Carolyn Nichols
Editor
LOVESWEPT
Bantam Books
666 Fifth Avenue
New York, NY 10103